"Don't judge everybody by your standards! We don't all sleep around."

Bianca flinched at the contempt in Matt's voice, the coldness in his gaze.

"I just told you, I'm not—don't..." she stammered.

"I know, you're just one of Don Heston's executives!"

"It's true!"

"But Don thinks he owns you. Why should he think you were likely to be with me all night? Did he tell you to get me to sign this contract by seducing me?"

CHARLOTTE LAMB was born in London, England, in time for World War II, and spent most of the war moving from relative to relative to escape bombing. Educated at a convent, she married a journalist, and now has five children. The family lives on the Isle of Man. Charlotte Lamb has written over a hundred books for Harlequin Presents®.

Books by Charlotte Lamb

HARLEQUIN PRESENTS®
2046—HOT SURRENDER
2070—THE YULETIDE CHILD

Don't miss any of our special offers. Write to us at the following address for information on our newest releases.

Harlequin Reader Service
U.S.: 3010 Walden Ave., P.O. Box 1325, Buffalo, NY 14269
Canadian: P.O. Box 609, Fort Erie, Ont. L2A 5X3

CHARLOTTE LAMB

The Seduction Business

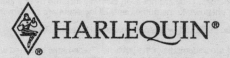

TORONTO • NEW YORK • LONDON
AMSTERDAM • PARIS • SYDNEY • HAMBURG
STOCKHOLM • ATHENS • TOKYO • MILAN • MADRID
PRAGUE • WARSAW • BUDAPEST • AUCKLAND

ISBN 0-373-12085-0

THE SEDUCTION BUSINESS

First North American Publication 2000.

CHAPTER ONE

THERE were four men and two women gathered in the boardroom by ten o'clock that bright May morning. They took their seats around the wide mahogany table occupying the centre of the room, in order of seniority and custom. The sales director, Jack Rowe, in the centre, looked pointedly at his watch. 'He's late. You'd think he'd be early today, of all days, wouldn't you?'

'He's been on the phone non-stop since eight o'clock,' the publicity officer, Noelle Hyland, said sharply, resenting the other man's tone. She leaned forward to stare at Jack with dislike, her spiky hair bright gold in the sunlight, making her look like a blonde hedgehog, especially as she was wearing a dark grey knitted wool suit which had a faintly fuzzy look to it.

'He looks dead tired,' said the female personnel director, Andrea Watson, sighing. Plump and cuddly in a pink angora sweater and white skirt, she also resented Jack Rowe's carping over their managing director, to whom she was totally loyal.

Normally she smiled a lot, was full of fun, warm-hearted, enjoying life. Today, like her colleagues, she was serious, worried, a little pale.

Pausing in the doorway, Matt Hearne surveyed them before they noticed his arrival. Was one of them a Judas, ready to sell him and his company out?

Somebody inside the firm had to be involved, his lawyer, Leigh Hampton, had said to him ten minutes ago. 'You must have a Trojan Horse there, Matt—find out who it is and get rid of them fast.'

Matt did not want to believe it.

His bright blue eyes skimmed their faces, wishing he could read them like a balance sheet. If only human beings were that easy. How many of them had secretly been offered jobs if this take-over went through?

Anger burnt deep inside his chest. He had worked hard to build this firm up; it had been his life for ten years. He had put everything he had and was into it.

Now someone was trying to take it away from him.

Well, they weren't going to succeed, no matter what he had to do to stop them. He would never have thought of himself as a ruthless man, but he could become one, if he had to. He believed you could always do what you had to.

He walked forward and the others all looked up, immediately alert, trying to read his expression to find out how he felt.

Andrea gave him a trusting, hopeful smile. She thought he was brilliant. Utterly wonderful. Cleverer than any man she had ever met, and sexy with it. Even though she was happily married with ten-year-old twins, Matt could make her heart flutter. Her husband, Gary, had noticed her watching Matt at a dinner party last winter, her eyes glowing with admiration, and teased her.

'You're wasting your time, love. Computers turn him on, not women. What makes you females go dreamy over the guy, anyway? What's he got that I haven't got?'

'Nothing, darling, not a thing,' she had quickly said, because the last thing she wanted to do was hurt Gary's feelings. But the truth was that although she loved her tall, burly husband, even in his old torn jeans and rugby shirt, gardening on a Sunday and covered in mud and grass-stains, Matt was gorgeous; more like a film star than a boss. Every other female in the office thought the same. She knew Noelle adored him. In fact, she had never yet met a woman who didn't love his warm, blue eyes, that pale brown, floppy, silky hair, his lazy, charming smile, and laid-back, lounging way of walking.

At lunchtime, in the coffee shop next door to the company's offices, where they all ate salads and jacket potatoes, the women who worked for him spent hours talking about how sexy Matt Hearne was and wishing he would look their way.

He never did.

There had been no woman in Matt's life at all since his wife, Aileen, died three years ago, giving birth to a premature baby girl. Andrea had seen Matt the next day and been shocked by how old he suddenly looked. His marriage had been a very happy one. He and Aileen had known each other from their school days. Aileen's death had hit him badly. She had tried to comfort him, but he had said brusquely, 'You're very kind, but I don't want to talk about it, Andrea.'

White, drawn, haggard, he had walked away and hadn't been seen in the offices for ten days. When he'd come back he was a different man. From then on he had buried himself in his work. He had lost a lot of weight, hardly spoke, became grim and taciturn.

Everyone had been worried about him, but a hardness in his eyes made them all afraid to say a word. Matt the charming, Matt the light-hearted had become surly and dangerous. They were scared of him for months.

Thank heavens, that harshness had slowly died away.

Over the past couple of years, to their relief, he had gradually returned to his old self. He laughed again, smiled often, chatted to them all casually, was approachable again, but in the blue eyes somewhere the shadow of heartbreak remained when he did not think he was being watched.

Andrea had often seen him gazing out over the steel-grey River Thames, below his office, his face set in lines of sadness, and wished she could say or do something to lighten his mood, but was afraid to offer comfort in case he bit her head off again.

'Good morning, everyone, thank you for being so punctual,' he said now, taking his own chair at the head of the table, facing his executives. 'I won't waste your time with a long preamble. We all know why we're here. Somebody has been buying up our shares. We've had a couple of near-misses in the past so we know the signs of a take-over bid. It's obviously a serious attack. They're spending a lot of money. I've asked Rod to find out everything he can. We'll hear him first, then I'd like each of you to give me your own personal opinion on the offer, before we settle back to discuss tactics. Okay?'

'Have they been in touch with you, Matt?' asked Jack Rowe, his face tight with nerves.

Shaking his head, Matt said, 'Not yet, but no doubt they soon will. I'm afraid these are big boys. Tell them who we're up against this time, Rod.'

'TTO,' Rod Cadogan said.

Nobody looked surprised, Matt noted wryly. They had already heard that Tesmost Technical Operations were behind the bid, no doubt. You couldn't keep such matters secret. Theirs was a small world. All the big international electronics firms knew each other. Several had tried to buy Hearne's in the last two years, since it leaked out that they were working on a cheap voice-operated computer. In this business new technology was the name of the game. You had to keep launching new ideas or you died. Matt had kept his research a secret for as long as possible, not talking to anyone but his closest colleagues, but sooner or later he had had to start building the actual computer, which meant far more people getting involved in the project, and once that happened the word was out and the vultures gathered.

He had had the money to beat off all previous interest, but TTO were an enormous company with far more capital than Matt could put together. If Matt borrowed money to help him in this struggle, he would lose control of his company, anyway, to whoever lent the cash.

Bleakly, Matt wished he could work out how to defeat this bid without asking for help from anyone. But he knew he was between the devil and the deep blue sea. Maybe he should sell the house in the Essex countryside which he and Aileen had bought when they got married?

He lived in his London flat which was just the right size for a bachelor, very convenient for work, and surrounded by restaurants and shops. But his mother and his baby daughter lived in the Essex house, only an hour's drive away so that he could visit them often. When Aileen died his mother had moved into their home to take care of Lisa and the arrangement had worked so well that it had become a routine.

Darkness veiled his eyes. Sometimes he could not believe she was gone, gone for ever. Aileen had been so full of life; he could see her now, laughing at him, the wind of the Essex coast in her hair, her eyes loving.

Salt coated his throat.

He mustn't think of her. Stop it, he told himself. No looking back. Think about the future.

Well, if he had to sell the house he would sell his flat, too, and find somewhere big enough for his mother and the baby, too. Maybe it was time they all lived together? Having a split household like this wasn't natural. He ought to see more of Lisa now that she was becoming a little girl, not just a baby.

'You see, Matt, this is a well organised attack!' he suddenly heard, and, starting, came back to the present, to look at Rod.

Matt nodded. 'I'm afraid so.'

Rod sighed heavily. 'I've got a list of share transfers that have already been shifted by the big investors, the pension funds and companies.' In his flat London accent Rod began to read his list out like someone reading the names of mourners at a funeral.

He paused, looked up, said grimly, 'And in charge of organising the bid, and co-ordinating the buying in of major company shares, Bianca Milne, Forward Planning Director of TTO.' Rod placed a large colour photo on the desk and everyone stared down at it.

Jack Rowe gave a low wolf whistle. 'Hey, I could go for her!'

Andrea felt a quiver of envy. If only she looked like that! She would swap her own brown hair for that sleek, smooth blonde chignon any time, and as for that face… Oh, it wasn't fair. Some women had it all.

Matt had heard of Bianca Milne, but had never actually set eyes on her. He leaned forward and picked up the photograph, his mouth twisting.

'Not my type at all, Jack, and I'd hazard a guess you wouldn't get anywhere with her, either. She's the don't-touch-me type—look at those eyes. Cold as ice.'

Andrea's smile spread. He was so good at reading character in a glance!

'How old is she?' somebody asked. 'She looks too young to be heading a take-over bid.'

'She's not as young as she looks,' said Rod. 'She'll be thirty in a month or so, it seems.'

'I call that young,' Jack said gloomily. 'Wish I was thirty next month.'

'Married?' Andrea asked, hopefully.

Rod shook his head. 'No. And currently without a man. Gossip has it that her last relationship was with Lord Mistell's son, young Harry Mistell, who worked for one of the merchant banks her company supplied with the latest electronic hardware.'

Matt's eyes lifted to consider Rod's face. 'Who broke off the affair, her or him?'

'Her. They earned millions out of that deal, and Bianca Milne handled the sale. She stopped seeing young Mistell a few weeks later.'

Matt did not look surprised. He just nodded.

'She was dating him just to make the sale?' Noelle said, frowning. 'That's horrible.'

Rod shrugged. 'Whether she was using him, or their break-up was a coincidence, who knows? But that's how the gossip goes. She's been with TTO for nine years, climbed rapidly up the company. The way she looks must have helped, but apparently she's also clever, tough and very ambitious. She has a strong power base there. There is a rumour that she has a secret affair going with Don Heston, the chief executive of the company, but again I don't know how true that is.' Rod paused, added softly, 'Heston is married.'

'And has kids,' said Matt and Rod nodded.

'Two, a boy and a girl in their teens. Heston is nearly

fifty, but looks younger. Nobody ever sees his wife. She stays in the country with the kids—they've got a big house in Buckinghamshire. Heston mostly jets around the world. Bianca Milne often goes with him.'

'Hence the rumours, of course,' Matt said briskly. 'And who could blame him if he did mix business with pleasure with someone who looks like that? Okay, give us the background on TTO's current market position, Rod. Concentrate, everyone. We need to find any chinks in their armour, any weaknesses. I'll set up a meeting with Heston in the next few days to find out what sort of war this is going to be.'

His eyes fell on the photograph again. Bianca Milne had a cool, remote, Madonna-like face—but what sort of mind lay behind those big green eyes? A woman more ruled by her head than her heart, obviously.

Matt thought of his dead wife, who had been warm and funny and sweet, a woman ruled by her heart, never her head. God, he missed her. Day and night. Especially at night when his bed was cold and empty.

Pulling himself up, he pushed his memories away, staring at the photo of Bianca Milne. Rumours didn't come from nowhere. Had she slept with Lord Mistell's son just to get that contract? Was that the sort of woman she was? Rod had heard she was Heston's mistress as well as his right-hand woman.

The girl with that purity of countenance and coldness of eye must have a few weaknesses, which could be useful to know. And maybe she was Heston's weakness? It could be even more useful to know that.

Bianca was dictating to her secretary when Don rang. 'Ready?'

He rarely wasted words or time. She wasn't surprised by his curt tone.

Looking at her watch, Bianca was surprised, however, to realise it was already twelve o'clock. It had been a busy morning; she had lost track of time, deep in concentration, trying to get as much work as possible done before she left for this very important lunch appointment.

'Yes, of course. I'll see you downstairs in two minutes.'

Don rang off in his usual curt fashion and Bianca quickly finished dictating.

'Get those into the computer, and printed, Patricia, and I'll sign them before I go home tonight.'

Patricia stood up, her shorthand pad in one hand, checking the pages of notes, the number of letters to be done, her face gloomy at the thought of all that work. She was a small, dark girl who didn't really enjoy her job. She had been engaged for six months and was counting the days to her wedding, after which, she'd frankly told Bianca, she meant to have a family as soon as possible and give up work for ever.

Bianca had drily said, 'What an old-fashioned attitude. Two incomes are better than one, you know, especially during the first year or so of a marriage. Can you afford to give up work and live on one salary?'

But it seemed that Patricia's future husband was a financial analyst who earned six times what Patricia could earn. Her income would not be important to them.

Smiling smugly, Patricia had told her, 'We don't have to worry about money; Tony earns more than enough for two and he wants to have kids as much as I do. He's thirty-five, his biological clock is ticking loudly. So is mine. I love kids and I want to have a lovely house and garden. That has always been my ambition. I've never been married to my job, you know, the way you are.'

'Yes, I've noticed you don't enjoy your job,' Bianca had said flatly. 'Let's hope you enjoy being a housewife. I think you'll discover housework isn't exactly fun, either. Well, give me plenty of notice so that I can find a replacement for you.'

Next time she meant to make sure she got a livewire secretary who put a bit more into her job, enjoyed what she did; not a lacklustre girl only interested in clothes, her own appearance and her private life.

Walking to the door now, Patricia asked over her shoulder, 'What time do you think you'll get back from lunch?'

'No idea. It depends how the Hearne people react. We could have a short, nasty exchange and break up early. Or we could go on all afternoon. Just make sure those letters are ready for me to sign when I get back.'

Sniffing pointedly, Patricia went out and Bianca went over to the mirror on her wall to check on her appearance. Fortunately there were no hairs out of place in her blonde chignon, so she did not need to touch that, but her pale pink lipstick needed to be renewed, and there was a faint sheen of perspiration on her nose and temples, so she swiftly brushed loose powder over her foundation.

Appearance was half the battle with some men. She had researched Matt Hearne for some months, and knew he didn't have a reputation as a lady-killer, but if he was like most men he would be staring at her while they talked and she wanted to make the right impression.

Her very feminine colouring, delicate-featured oval

face and slender figure were in startling contrast to the businesslike navy blue pinstripe suit she was wearing.

She dressed that way whenever she had an important business meeting. In the beginning men had taken one look and begun talking indulgently, condescendingly, as though blonde hair and big green eyes must mean she was a ninny.

In her job, that male attitude was a nuisance. It wasted valuable time. It was boring having to fend off passes, and irritating that men did not take her seriously.

She had tried various ways of making men treat her with respect as a colleague or an opponent, and had found that wearing a man's suit worked best.

It presented a conflicting visual impression which left men uncertain how to treat her, put them off their stride long enough for Bianca to have time to convince them she was no airhead and they should listen to her as attentively as they would listen to a man.

She collected her elaborately presented folder from the desk, glanced through it to make sure she had everything she would need, slid it into her black leather briefcase, before walking out to the lift on the landing outside her office.

TTO occupied most of this new, modern, luxury office block in the City of London. The offices in which Don Heston and his team of secretaries and assistants worked was on the thirtieth floor. Above that lay the roof garden, where they sometimes held summer barbecues for the staff, sunbathed, ate their sandwiches. On the same level was the elegant, expensively furnished apartment Don kept for himself or visiting VIPs from other countries in the world who did not want to stay in hotels.

He was waiting for her in his long black limousine

on the forecourt of the building. A large, rugged man with curly brown hair sprinkled with silver, and hard, piercing brown eyes, he looked younger than he was because he worked out in the gym each day, played golf, swam, watched his diet and wore expensive, designer fashion in the latest styles.

Sliding into the back seat beside him, Bianca pretended not to notice as he ran his usual acquisitive stare over her.

'You're late.'

Her face was calm and unworried by the snapped accusation. 'Sorry, Don. I was dictating when you rang.'

'Done all your homework on this deal?'

'Of course.'

He gave her a satisfied nod. 'Good girl.' Casually he shifted nearer till his knee touched hers, his eyes still roving over her from head to toe. 'You know, that outfit should be a passion-killer—I usually hate to see women dressing as men—but you manage to look sexier than ever in it. Let's hope Hearne thinks so; it would be very useful if he fell for you the way young Mistell did.'

She bit her inner lip. She did not want to remember Harry.

Don's arm slid along the top of the seat behind her. Bianca felt his fingers trickle over her bare nape and stiffened.

'Don't,' she muttered, not wishing his chauffeur to hear her, and moved forward to escape Don's caress, relieved when his hand fell away from her skin and slipped back to his side, but his thigh was still close to hers as the car drove off.

He had been making passes at her ever since she started working for him, but so far she had always managed to keep him at bay. She knew he had had affairs with other women in the company and she had no intention of becoming one of that long list. But Don was a tenacious, determined man who never gave up and when he met a denial simply took a breath then came back again on the offensive. He never missed an opportunity to press an advantage, and never gave up.

It was irritating, but Bianca did not want to slap him down too hard. She respected Don's brains, and liked him. But he was married, and as the child of divorced parents she hated the very idea of breaking up a marriage. She had rarely seen his wife and did not really know her at all. He was obviously no family man. He rarely seemed to be at his country home. Bianca was far too discreet to comment, but she remembered her own childhood well enough to know how his long absences must upset his children.

She enjoyed her job running the department which was actively engaged in seeking companies which the company could acquire with advantage. Bianca had to have a sound knowledge of the market values, the sometimes hidden assets of a company, the future potential which they would also often hide from acquisitive eyes.

Don gave her the sort of responsibility and power she had always dreamt of but never dared hope she would achieve. Women were rarely allowed to climb to the very top in business. This was still largely a man's world. She knew she owed her chance to develop her financial skills to Don and was grateful to him.

Oh, no doubt he assumed she would pay the price he set on her job, but he hadn't, so far, turned nasty when she refused to give in to his blatant desire for her.

'Frigid little cat,' he said now, but grinned as he said

it, because he didn't believe she was anything of the
kind and still hoped to get her one of these days.

He had watched from the sidelines as she got involved with Harry; calculating that her relationship with
Harry would help push through the deal with Lord
Mistell, who adored his only son. The relationship had
broken up when Harry heard gossip about her being
Don's mistress. Bianca had tried to make Harry believe
it was all a lie, but he wouldn't listen. White-faced and
angry he had walked out of her life that night and she
had not set eyes on him since.

'You're a married man, Don, and I'm not breaking
up your marriage.'

'I've told you—ours has always been a free and easy
marriage. I go my way, she goes hers! Sara's life is
very busy; she has the children, her home, her dogs, the
charity committees she works for—there wouldn't even
be room for me if I lived there full time.'

Bianca grimaced, wondering how true that was, but
answering coolly, 'The way you run your marriage is
your business, but I am not the free and easy type. I
don't go in for adultery, it's too messy.'

He laughed shortly. 'You're too old-fashioned to be
true! But Matt Hearne is a widower, remember, and as
free as the birds.'

'This is a business lunch! You don't expect me to
use sex to get Matt Hearne to sign over his business, I
hope!'

'Use whatever works,' said Don, sounding highly
amused. 'How many times have I told you that there's
no place for morals in business? The bottom line is
money. Nothing else counts.'

'Don't be so cynical!'

'I'm rational, not cynical. If we can get hold of

Hearne's new technology we'll be coining money soon. It's essential we get Hearne himself, though. He's a genius. None of our researchers can touch him. We want him as well as his company.'

'Then you talk him into signing!'

Don changed tack. 'You know, the man must be pretty lonely. Since his wife died he hasn't been seen with anyone else, I gather. That must mean he's in need of some good sex, so I want you to be nice to him. Very, very nice, Bianca. If you know what I mean— and of course you do!' He laughed uproariously.

She gave him an icy stare. 'You may think that's funny, Don, but I don't! I'm not sleeping with him just to get him to sign that contract!' Anger made the hair stir on the back of her neck. 'Sex may be your answer to everything, but it isn't mine. I have too much self-respect.'

They turned into the Savoy Hotel courtyard and the limousine slowed to a stop in front of the swing doors. The uniformed commissionaire moved forward to open the passenger door for Bianca to descend, so she leashed in her temper again as she got out of the car. She couldn't have a row with her boss in front of a fascinated audience.

'You've got no sense of humour,' he murmured, following her through the hotel's swing doors. 'Lighten up, sweetheart! And keep smiling. We want to get Hearne's signature on that contract, remember!'

Matt Hearne and a couple of his executives had already arrived, they were told, and were waiting in the River Room bar, sitting right in front of one of the famous art nouveau mirrors, with their coloured urns of flowers reflecting the light of the great chandeliers in the centre of the room.

'There's Hearne,' Don said, striding forward, past the white piano occupying the centre of the long, wide room.

Bianca kept pace with him, aware of three pairs of eyes fixed on her but looking past them, into the mirror behind them. Her reflection moved to meet her in flowing graceful strides: the smooth blonde hair, the oval face, and then the pinstriped jacket, open to reveal the sexy way her waistcoat fitted her high breasts and slender waist. Across the front of it swung a gold watch-chain, moving with every step her long legs took.

She looked calmer than she felt. Don had made her angry and agitated, she was breathing too quickly, her colour high.

The waiting men rose to greet them. 'Good to see you again, Matt,' Don said, holding out his hand to one of them.

'Hi, Don,' the other man drawled lightly and derisively. Don was not one of his favourite people, Bianca instantly picked up, but then he wouldn't be, would he? Matt Hearne had founded his own company which Don was now trying to acquire. They were hardly going to be friends.

Don introduced her a second later. Matt Hearne's hand swallowed her own. His skin was cool, his grip firm but brief.

Bianca had seen photos of him but they had not prepared her for his physical presence, nor for the instant awareness of him she felt.

He had... She hesitated for the right description, then settled for magnetism. Yes, that was what he had. It glimmered in those bright, blue, mocking eyes. This was a man with charisma as well as sharp intelligence.

This was a moment she always felt deeply—the first

seconds of a duel, facing the opponent over their drawn swords.

Sometimes you knew you would easily win. It was going to be a push-over.

But not this man. He was no push-over.

He introduced his colleagues, who shook hands, staring at her in a way that was familiar but still irritating. Why couldn't men treat a woman as if she was a human being first and a female second? Why did they always look like that, as if they were imagining you naked?

A faint flush deepened on her cheeks. Would they look at each other like that? Of course they wouldn't.

The formalities over, they all sat down again and a waiter appeared.

'What will you have to drink, Bianca?' Don asked, playing the attentive host. He was paying for this meal, the three other men were TTO's guests, which Don felt gave him the advantage, and he always looked for a chance to get the advantage when he was making a deal. Don was a bridge player, a man with a sharp, quick, clever mind but very little heart.

When Bianca hesitated, Don said, 'How about champagne? Shall we all have some?' He glanced at the waiter and nodded. The waiter vanished.

'How is your wife, Don? I met her a couple of years ago at a party,' Matt Hearne said in a soft, deliberate voice.

Don looked blank. 'Did you? I wasn't there?'

'No,' agreed Matt Hearne, his blue eyes drifting over to scan Bianca's face in a way she resented. 'You weren't. Too busy elsewhere, I suppose?'

Bianca stiffened. Was she imagining the pointed tone? What was he hinting at?

'It was a charity function,' Matt murmured. 'Your

wife was involved in raising funds for Czech orphans. A very nice lady with a lovely smile.'

Yes, Bianca was sure he was needling Don, quite deliberately, and from Don's sudden frown he knew it.

Surely there hadn't been anything between Matt Hearne and Don's wife?

The waiter returned with an ice bucket and two bottles of champagne. They all watched him set out champagne glasses. He opened one bottle, and filled the glasses.

'To our closer understanding,' Don said to Matt Hearne, raising his glass, smiling again, all warmth and friendliness.

Nothing would ever interfere between Don and the making of money. Until he had achieved his deal he could put aside desire, rage, personal hatreds—any and every emotion. He had tunnel vision to an extraordinary degree.

She wondered if Matt Hearne was the same. He had been intensely successful; he and Don must have a lot in common.

'Oh, I already understand you, Don, don't worry,' Matt said, raising his glass, too, in Don's direction, and again she heard the hidden note of mockery.

Don's smile was tight, his teeth white and pointed. 'Good, I'm glad you do. I must say, your company is a little jewel, Matt, and I won't hide the fact that I want it. And what I want I always get.'

His eyes wandered on to touch Bianca, and she felt the insistence throbbing inside him, and tensed, her hands clenched at her sides.

Sometimes he was positively scary.

It was a difficult occasion from that moment. Oh, the

men smiled a great deal, but the hidden weapons each carried showed more and more as the lunch progressed.

How well did they know one another? wondered Bianca, watching them both. Were they older acquaintances than Don had ever told her?

She became very curious but could pick up no real clues to whatever lay in the past.

TTO had bought up over a third of the Hearne stock, which would mean that they inevitably had a considerable impact on future policy and planning in the company. But they had not yet managed to acquire control. Matt Hearne held too many shares and would not sell. His sister controlled a number of shares, too. Rumour had it that she and her brother weren't speaking. If they had seriously quarrelled and TTO could persuade her to sell they would get control.

The problem was, Ann Hearne had moved to the States a year ago and nobody seemed to know her address. Bianca had tried to find her and failed.

At present, they had a very good private detective over there looking for her. If they could find her in time, and persuade her to sell her shares to them, it would make the take-over much easier.

Watching Matt Hearne as they ate lunch—a game consommé under a pastry case, then turbot stuffed with a pink prawn mousse, and served with a selection of young fresh vegetables—Bianca wondered if his sister looked like him. If she had his colouring and grace Anne Hearne would undoubtedly be lovely.

As if feeling her eyes on his profile Matt turned his head as the waiter whipped their plates away. His blue eyes narrowed, gleamed. Something in that look made her flush and look away, her pulses quickening, which surprised her.

Don was watching them, a secret, satisfied smile curling his full mouth. She gave him an icy look. If he thought she would fall in with his plans for her and Matt Hearne he could think again.

The tense discussions resumed, with stubborn resistance from the Hearne camp. They were going to fight TTO all the way, Bianca realised, but then what had Don expected?

Over coffee and liqueurs Don suddenly said, 'Clearly we need to have some more meetings. I'm going to Australia in a couple of days, but Bianca will be...' A deliberate pause, then he added, 'Available.'

Matt Hearne glanced at her, raising a brow, cool assessment in his eyes.

Biting her lip, she looked down. She couldn't blame him for reading what he clearly did from the way Don had said that. What else was he to think?

Just what Don had meant him to think, in fact.

'Who else will I be talking to?' Matt drawled.

'Oh, just Bianca,' said Don softly. 'The two of you can come to terms more agreeably than a whole bunch of guys fighting it out, don't you agree?'

Burning with indignation, her eyes lowered because she couldn't trust herself not to burst out in white-hot fury, which would probably destroy any hope of a deal, Bianca listened to Matt Hearne saying, 'Then why don't we start with dinner tomorrow night? If you're free, Bianca?'

'She'll be delighted, won't you, Bianca?' Don didn't let her speak for herself in case she made up some excuse. 'What time and where?'

'How about my flat?' Matt Hearne drawled. 'We can't talk seriously in a restaurant—too many ears and eyes. We don't want the media picking up on our talks. Eight o'clock?'

Don quickly said, 'Eight o'clock, your flat—that's in Chelsea, isn't it? We have the address. Bianca will be there.'

'I shall look forward to it,' Matt Hearne said, and Bianca looked up then, meeting his amusement, hating him for the contempt and mockery in that gaze, dying to tell him to get lost but knowing Don would be furious if she did.

Don called for the bill and paid it with his credit card, then got up hastily. 'Sorry, we have to rush now. Pressure of work, you know how it is! It's been a pleasure, Matt.'

He took Bianca's arm in a tight grip and pulled her out of her chair, propelled her away from the table.

'How could you do that?' she snapped as they walked back up into the foyer. 'You practically offered me on a plate! What do you imagine he's thinking?'

Don chuckled. 'All you have to do is lead him up the garden path until he signs. That was what you did with young Mistell. I'm not asking you to go to bed with Hearne. Just let him think you might.'

She turned to stare at him, her green eyes glittering like broken glass, her skin burning. She couldn't remember the last time she had felt this angry. She had known for a long time that Don was a cynic—why did his latest attempt to manipulate her make her so furious?

She knew very well, of course. She had hated the way Matt Hearne looked at her just now. It hurt to imagine him despising her.

'I don't believe I heard that. No, Don, I will not do it. And I did not lead Harry on.'

'Were you in love with him?' Don pointedly asked, and she hesitated.

'I liked him a lot.'

'But you weren't in love, were you? I've known you a long time, Bianca, I've watched you date guys for a while then end it. I'm curious—have you ever been in love?'

'Mind your own business.'

'You haven't, have you?' He smiled in satisfaction. 'I don't believe you're totally ice-bound. Somewhere under the ice there's fire, and I want to be the one to reach it.'

She gave him a scathing glance. 'No chance, Don. No chance at all.'

He laughed. 'We'll see. As for Hearne, if you won't even flirt with him at least be friendly. Courtesy costs nothing, does it? This is a business meeting. You can set the tone; you're not stupid. And he doesn't look the type to turn nasty, does he?'

No, she conceded silently. But men were often un-predictable and she was not comfortable with the pros-pect of having dinner alone with Matt Hearne in his flat. After what Don had said to him he might well think she was part of whatever deal they offered him.

She would ring him tomorrow and suggest they have dinner in a restaurant.

CHAPTER TWO

THE news that the two companies had had lunch together at the Savoy appeared in several morning newspapers, next day, and the press kept the phone lines busy all morning, but no statement was issued by either firm.

Bianca worked with Don for several hours, before he flew to Australia, to tie up loose ends of various projects they had in hand. He went off to lunch with some of the other executives, leaving her at her desk with a pile of paperwork to read through, so when the office lunch trolley came round she bought a yogurt, an apple and some cheese.

Patricia, however, said she had a lunch date with her fiancé, and went out, abandoning the letters she had to type, to Bianca's irritation. She continued to work, eating her lunch at the same time, which was why when her phone rang she had her mouth full of cheese and apple.

As Patricia wasn't around she picked it up, murmuring, 'Mmm?' between chews.

'I would like to speak to Bianca Milne.' She recognised the voice before he added, 'My name is Matthew Hearne.'

Flushed, and hurriedly swallowing the food, she finally managed to say thickly, 'This is Bianca Milne. Hello, Mr Hearne.'

'Matt,' he said, a smile sounding in his voice. 'Are you having lunch at your desk?'

Startled and pink, she mumbled, 'Er…yes, actually.' Had it been that obvious?

'Snap. So am I. What are you having?'

'A Greek yogurt, a Cox's apple and a piece of Cheddar,' she said, hoping she didn't sound as flustered as she felt.

'That sounds much better than my ham and pickle sandwich. Is your boss there?'

'I'm sorry, he's out.'

'No desk-bound lunch for him, eh? I suppose he's having a rich lunch somewhere special, with lots of wine. How does he work after that?'

'Don doesn't drink much,' she lied. Not much he didn't. 'Do you want him to ring you when he gets back, Mr Hearne?'

'No, it was you I wanted to talk to. I picked up the impression that you weren't too keen on the idea of eating at my flat tonight.'

She was silent—how did she answer that politely?

He laughed softly. 'So why don't I book dinner in a good restaurant? Any preferences?'

'No,' she said with relief. 'I'll leave the choice to you.'

'Okay. I'll pick you up at seven at your flat. See you then.'

'My address is…' she began, her words trailing into silence as she realised he had already hung up. That must mean he already knew her address. Well, she knew his, so why should she be surprised about that? No doubt his people had been very busy checking her and Don out ever since their hit began. It didn't worry her because she had no secrets to hide; however deep they dug his investigators wouldn't find out anything they could use against her. Don was another story. Who knew what secrets he had to hide?

He came into her room at five-thirty that day, as charged up as usual, and barked at her. 'Still here? Go home now and make yourself beautiful for Hearne.'

She leaned back in her chair, her body giving a weary but graceful stretch in the clinging grey jersey dress she wore.

'I will, soon. What time's your flight for Sydney tomorrow?'

'First thing, God help me. Now, keep me informed of how your talks with Hearne go, won't you?'

'Of course. Fax or phone?'

'Phone. Faxes are too risky for this one—other people will read them before I do. I'll ring you at home in the evening from my hotel, okay? That way we can be fairly sure we aren't being overheard.' He turned to go, said over his shoulder, 'And, Bianca, you won't wear anything as boring as that dress, will you? I want you to knock Hearne for six and have him putty in your hand by the time I get back.'

She glared after him. 'I'll be polite to the man, I don't promise anything else!'

Bianca arrived home half an hour later having taken a taxi instead of her usual underground train. The office was close to a tube station and so was her home—a spacious flat on the top floor of a large Victorian house in Pimlico, just a street or two away from Pimlico underground station. From the high bay windows of her sitting room she had a view across gardens bright with spring flowers to the river. Her bedroom overlooked the back of the house; a large magnolia tree grew right outside, the delicate pale pink candle-like flowers just below her windowsill.

She opened the window to air the room and a wonderful scent of wallflowers and stocks floated in. Whenever she got home she felt peace descend on her. She had taken a good deal of trouble to give her flat a tranquil feeling—soft, soothing pale colours, landscapes hanging on the walls, a waist-high bookcase running halfway round the sitting room, a good stereo music centre where she played her favourite CDs when she was alone each evening, pretty lamps here and there shedding low light, a spacious, open feel to the rooms. This was where she unwound after the tensions and pressures of the day at work. This was where she could be alone, at ease, untroubled.

Don had never been invited, although he often dropped hints about wanting to see her home. She did not want the atmosphere ruined for her by memories of Don making a pass, or talking in his assertive, ruthless fashion about work.

First, she glanced through the mail waiting for her— a bill, a home shopping catalogue, a postcard. She knew who it was from as soon as she saw the picture on the front. Lake Como was where her father now lived. She read the few sentences in his large, black, sprawling handwriting. He was well and so was Maria, his second wife, and their son, Lorenzo, who had been eight yesterday and sent Bianca his love. The weather was wonderful; he hoped she was well, too. It could have been a card sent by a mere acquaintance.

That was what it was, she thought bitterly—a few words from a virtual stranger. What did she know about her father? From the day he walked out on her and her mother Bianca had only seen him half a dozen times.

Why had he got in touch now? Had something reminded him she existed? Made him feel a little guilty?

Her mouth twisted icily. Well, he would soon forget her again. He always did. It would probably be years before she heard from him once more.

She dropped the card on the kitchen table and walked through to the bathroom to take a quick shower, then went to her bedroom, in her short black towelling robe, to put on a black bra and panties, then a matching, filmy black slip. Clicking through the clothes in her wardrobe, she finally picked out a simple black tunic dress, sleeveless, with a scoop neckline, and a hem just above the knee. If Matt Hearne should turn out to have expectations she had no intention of fulfilling it would help if she looked a trifle austere.

With her blonde hair swept up into a French pleat behind her head, tied there with a large black bow set with a diamanté clasp, her face smoothly made up, lips pale pink, lids brushed with green shadow which had a faint glitter to it, her reflection was elegant and cool.

Automatically she added a touch of her favourite French perfume on pulse points—at her wrists, behind her ears, in the hollow of her throat—then started violently as her front doorbell rang and spilled a little perfume on her dress and the carpet.

Groaning, she stoppered the bottle and put it back on the dressing table.

That's all I need—to smell like a brothel! she thought, brushing her dress and waving her arms about to disperse the strong smell of perfume.

Why did he have to be early? She wasn't ready to cope with him yet; she needed more time.

Why am I so nervous? she wondered, staring into the mirror and seeing a darkness, an anxiety in her eyes.

She had had so many business dinners and lunches with men, in the past, both alone and with Don. Why was it different this time? Pull yourself together! she told her reflection. He's just another man. Nothing is different. You can deal with Matt Hearne.

He rang the doorbell again. Bianca dragged a cool mask over her face, took a deep breath, turned and picked up her purse and a warm cashmere wrap, because although it had been a warm spring day it was chillier now, and went to open the door.

She found him leaning casually against the wall outside, long and lean and elegant in tailor-made evening clothes, which made him look even taller, slimmer, his waist clipped by the smooth-fitting waistcoat, those very long legs smoothly encased in dark trousers, a white carnation in his buttonhole.

Bianca's breath caught in her throat. Why did he have to be so attractive?

'I was beginning to suspect you'd forgotten I was coming,' he drawled, those cynical blue eyes flickering all over her, making a strange, hot pulse start to beat inside her body.

What is the matter with me? she angrily asked herself. She must stop behaving like a schoolgirl finding herself alone with a man for the first time in her life.

'Sorry,' she said tersely. 'You're early. I wasn't quite ready.'

'Are you ready now?' he queried, one brow lifting in teasing query, and she thought, No! I need more time. Go away; come back later. Maybe then I'll have got myself under control.

But she couldn't say that because it would betray a weakness and in this fight between them she must never let him imagine he could win. She had to stay in command, give the impression she was invulnerable, he wouldn't get anywhere with her.

It worried her that she was already having to struggle to keep her cool. Why did this man get under her skin, bother her so much? She had never felt this sort of reaction to anyone else. Oh, she had found men attractive, from time to time, but had always stayed calm, in control, had never felt this disturbing awareness before.

'Do you want me to come in and wait while you finish getting ready?' he offered.

'No!' she said, far too quickly, and saw amusement glint in his eyes. Crossly pulling the red cashmere wrap around her throat with hands that weren't quite steady, she said, 'I'm quite ready now, shall we go?'

She closed her front door; Matt Hearne stood back to allow her to go down the stairs first. In the communal hallway of the apartment block they met one of her neighbours, a young man in jeans and a vivid striped sweater, who gave her a smile, nodding.

'Hi, Bee.'

'Hello, Gary,' she said coldly, stalking past. A medical student at a London teaching hospital, he was the only son of wealthy parents who had spoilt him.

One night soon after he'd arrived he had come back drunk and tried to push his way into her flat. They had had quite a tussle until she managed to thrust him out and lock her door. He had banged for ten minutes before giving up and going downstairs. He had a studio flat at the back of the ground floor where he played heavy metal rock, far too loud, infuriating the other tenants, who would have had him evicted if the whole house had not been owned by one of Gary's doting aunts.

To do him credit, Gary had come up next day with a bunch of flowers and an apology, but Bianca had kept him at a distance ever since. She did not want a repeat performance of his attempt to get into her flat.

Matt Hearne gave her an amused look, asking softly, 'An admirer?'

'A nuisance,' was all she said, going out of the building.

A sleek white sports car was parked outside the gate, under the street lamp. Bianca eyed it appreciatively, slowing to stop beside it. 'Is that yours?'

He shot her a sideways glance. 'Do you like it?'

'Love it,' she said, wishing she owned it. It must cost a fortune, which would be right out of her reach. 'It looks very fast. What can it do?'

'A hundred and fifty, if I put my foot down.'

'Please don't, tonight,' she said.

He walked round to open the passenger door and held it open while she got into the car, eyeing her long legs with sensual appraisal. Bianca wished she had not worn such a short dress. Sitting down in the low-slung vehicle instantly made her skirt rise. Hurriedly, she smoothed her skirt down to her knees again while Matt Hearne watched, his mouth twitching with mocking enjoyment.

He shut the door at last and came round to get behind the wheel, his lean body gracefully adjusting to the driver's seat. His long legs almost touched hers, his left arm brushed her elbow, and she hurriedly jerked away. She was intensely conscious of being close to him in a very small space, of the light fragrance of whatever aftershave he was wearing, of his slow, calm breathing, his hands lightly resting on the wheel, the possibility of contact, of touching him.

Her mouth was suddenly dry. She stared at his hands—powerful, elegant, a sprinkle of dark hair on the backs of them, his long fingers shifting to start the car with a roar like a lion.

The silence was making her ears beat with hot blood.

As he drove off, fast, she swallowed and asked, 'Where are we going?'

'My favourite restaurant, Les Sylphides…it only opened this year but the cooking is marvellous. French provincial, with new twists. I hope you like French food?'

'I do,' she said. 'We often eat it. I'm surprised I've never heard of this place. I thought I knew every good restaurant in town.'

'This isn't really in town. It's on the edge of Epping Forest, at Loughton—do you know Essex?'

'Vaguely. Well, I know where it is, east of the city, but I've never actually been over there.'

'It's a very special place. Loughton was a village; now it's a growing suburb but still has a village atmosphere.'

'Will it take long to get there?' She had no real idea of the outskirts of London; she rarely left the centre of the city.

'Not at this time of night. Half an hour or so. And the great point is, we aren't likely to see anyone who knows either of us so we'll be able to talk without alerting anybody to what's going on.' He laughed curtly. 'Although, of course, there are whispers already. If you start buying up shares, forcing the price up, the market soon knows what's afoot. But as neither of our companies have given a statement to the press, so far the rumours are only that—rumours. The longer we can put off an announcement the better. It will only cloud the issue if we have the press on our backs.'

'I agree. We don't want press intervention, either.' Bianca stared out of the car at the faintly dirty, shabby streets through which they were driving. This was a part of London she had never seen before. 'Where are we now?' Scraps of torn paper, crumpled drink cans, fast-food boxes blew along the gutters, and there was an air of decay and indifference on all sides.

He gave her an odd look. 'Haven't you ever been here before? This is the East End.'

She should have guessed. 'Not very attractive, is it?'

'You may not think so. Over the last hundred years it has looked like heaven to the immigrants from Europe, the Jews who fled from Eastern Europe, during the twenties and thirties, and now the place is home to Pakistanis and West Indians, not to mention some streets where you find nothing but Cypriots, both Greek and Turkish, and Africans whose countries are caught up in civil war. There are so many ethnic shops and restaurants here, it is like the world in miniature.'

'Is Loughton like this?'

'No, Loughton is way out of town, and much of it has been built since the war.' He gave her one of his slow, amused smiles, and she couldn't help noticing his charm, a quality Don really did not share. 'You obviously aren't a Londoner.'

'No, I'm from the West Country...'

'Whereabouts?'

'Dorset, actually—Lyme Regis.'

'Ah, French Lieutenant's Woman territory.'

'That's the place. It's lovely.'

'Did you grow up looking for dinosaurs? Aren't there lots of them in the cliffs at Lyme Bay?'

'Well, lots of fossils, yes. And we did do expeditions to hunt for fossils, from school.'

'That would have prepared you for working for Don Heston. He's a bit of a fossil himself—into money-making for shareholders rather than creating jobs for people. The red-in-tooth-and-claw capitalist only cares about making money. A modern boss looks to making his company work for the people he employs, which means both making money and giving staff a good working environment.'

'Don is a very good boss, Mr Hearne.'

'Matt.'

She gave him a cool stare. 'Matt. Don is very go-ahead and modern. I couldn't ask to work for a better boss. He has encouraged me from the day I joined the firm.'

His long mouth curled mockingly. 'Yes, I noticed the interest he took in you.'

Coins of red appeared in her cheeks. 'What's that supposed to mean?'

'Don't try to tell me his interest is purely philan-thropic because I wouldn't believe you. You're lovely, and Don Heston wants you.'

'That's insulting! But then men like you think women are only good for one thing, don't you?'

'Oh, I think women are good for many things,' he drawled. 'We can talk about that later. For now, tell me how you got the job with Heston? Did he pick you out of the typing pool? I know I would have done.'

Frozen-faced, she bit out, 'No, I joined TTO straight from college.'

'Which one?'

'I went to the London School of Economics.'

'Oh, yes, I remember reading that you were at the LSE.'

'Don recruited me because my tutor was a friend of his and recommended me.'

They were driving through a suburb now, but as she stared out Matt Hearne slowed and queued up at what was clearly a motorway junction.

'The M11—this is a fast route to Loughton,' he told her as she looked around in some doubt. Where on earth was he taking her? How much further were they going? Before she could ask he said, 'Do you know Heston's wife?'

She gave him a wary look. Was he going to give her a third degree on the subject of Mrs Heston?

'Not really. I've met her once or twice, but she prefers to live in the country, with their children, whereas Don spends the week in town, in his flat, and only goes home at weekends.'

'From what Sara told me, he goes home very rarely.'

She turned to look at his profile and found it unusually sombre in the bright lightning flashes of the motorway light as they drove very fast along the outside lane. A lock of his light brown hair flopped over his temples; his mouth was straight, his jaw taut, his blue eyes hidden by drooping lids as he stared straight ahead.

'You know her well?' She had picked up something yesterday, at lunch. Don had been odd when Matt Hearne mentioned his wife and Bianca's instincts had prickled with a sense of something not being said.

'No, I only met her recently, but by a strange coincidence I found out she was at school with my wife.'

So that was it! thought Bianca. If Matt Hearne had loved his wife and still missed her it would have meant something important for him to meet an old schoolfriend of hers. What irony for Don to target Matt's firm soon afterwards!

'Sara Heston's a very special person.'

Had he seen her again, since that first meeting, or had there only been that one occasion?

'She deserves better than being married to Heston,'

Matt Hearne murmured, half to himself. 'But maybe you don't agree?'

Coldly, Bianca said, 'I don't know her, I have no opinion.' Except that no woman deserved to be married to a selfish bastard like Don, but she would not say that to him.

Don was her boss, nothing more. She preferred to stay out of his private life.

He made no comment on that, slowing down and moving over to leave the motorway. 'We're turning off here. It isn't far now.'

'I was beginning to wonder if we'd ever get there!'

They were out in the country a moment later, driving between hedges of hawthorn in white flower, a beaten crescent moon rising in the cloudless sky, touching the edge of a forest, giving the dark interior a mysterious gleam, silvering church spires, windows and the roofs of cottages.

'Magical,' murmured Bianca, and he gave her one of his slow, charming smiles. Her heart appeared to have developed a disturbing flutter. Or had she swallowed one of the moths that were flying around them as Matt slowed to take another corner?

Before he had completed the turn another car flashed past along the lane they were entering. The driver was going far too fast. Matt had to brake violently to avoid a collision. Bianca was flung forward and almost hit the dashboard; was held only by her seat belt.

'What an idiot!' Matt angrily said. 'Are you okay?' He moved closer, his face concerned, helping her to sit back again. 'You didn't hurt yourself, did you?'

'No, I'm fine,' she said huskily, her heart racing with shock. It couldn't be beating so fast just because this man had touched her?

He looked into her eyes with a slow, sensual gaze that made her pulses flicker and leap.

'You're out of breath,' he murmured, and her mouth went dry.

'Shock,' she said hoarsely.

He smiled. 'I feel the same.'

And neither of them was talking about the near-miss they had just had.

From between their seats a phone began to ring, making her nerves go haywire all over again. After a few seconds Matt slowly leaned down to pick up the receiver.

'Matt Hearne.' His voice was curt, breathless.

Bianca couldn't hear what was being said to him, but she saw his face changing. In the moonlight he suddenly looked pale, or was she imagining that? Was it just moonlight on his skin?

'How serious is it?'

Another pause while he listened, and he was definitely pale, his features tense.

'No!' he abruptly said. 'Please, don't do that. I am on my way now; I should be there in about half an hour. Could you stay there until I arrive? Leave her in bed; don't wake her up.'

He listened again, briefly, then said, 'Thank you, Mrs Morley. I'll get there as soon as humanly possible.'

He pushed the phone back down between the seats and started to drive much faster between the high, flowering hedges.

'Look, I'm sorry, Bianca, I have to cancel dinner. That was a neighbour ringing to tell me my mother has been taken to hospital with appendicitis and will be having an operation at once. But don't worry; I'll stop somewhere *en route* and find you a taxi to take you back to London.'

Quickly she protested, 'I can get a train. Don't worry about me. I hope your mother's operation is successful and she recovers quickly.'

'So do I,' he said in heartfelt tones. 'At the moment, it isn't just my mother I'm worrying about. My little girl is asleep upstairs in the house. The police wanted to take her off to a foster home for the night. I want to get there fast to stop that happening. She would be petrified. She's far too young to understand. All she would know was that strangers were taking her away from her home in the middle of the night.'

Bianca could imagine how scared the little girl would be, and why Matt wanted to make sure his child didn't have such a shock. 'How old is she?'

'Three.' The car roared on along the empty country lanes; he really had his foot down. She watched the needle flickering upwards; he was doing eighty miles an hour.

'Oh, poor baby!' Bianca said with sympathy. 'It would be a nightmare for her, wouldn't it? Couldn't your neighbour take care of her?'

He sighed. 'She's eighty years old. She couldn't possibly cope with Lisa. No, I shall have to collect her, take her back to my flat, and in the morning find someone to take care of her for the moment. The problem is, I want to go to the hospital, too, to see my mother, and I can hardly take Lisa with me. And tomorrow's Saturday; it won't be easy to find a temporary nanny during the weekend.'

'What about your sister? You do have a sister, don't you?'

He gave her a dry look. 'I imagine you've been looking for her in the hope of buying her shares. Yes, I have a sister, but I have no idea where she is at present. She's probably abroad somewhere.'

'Haven't you got a mother-in-law?'

'I had one, but she died last year. She never recovered from Aileen's death. She had a heart attack in bed one night and was found dead in the morning. And I have no other relatives to take Lisa, unhappily. Neither my wife nor I came from big families. But I can look after Lisa myself, tonight, although this comes at the worst possible time, with all the workload of the take-over to deal with.'

'I could look after her tonight,' offered Bianca before she even knew what she was going to say. Her mouth had opened of its own accord and out the words had popped. Instantly she realised what a stupid offer it had been. What did she know about taking care of small children? She had never had anything to do with children. Hadn't she got enough to do without taking on such a responsibility?

But it was too late to have second thoughts or doubts. Slowing down, Matt Hearne looked round into her eyes again, smiling.

'You're an angel. Thank you. That would be an enormous help.'

What have I done? she thought, staring back at him and smiling stupidly. I must be out of my mind. I'm probably going to regret this.

But ever since she'd heard about Matt Hearne's wife's death and the fact that his little girl lived apart from him, with his mother, she had felt a link, a strange sense of kinship, with the child.

CHAPTER THREE

THE lanes grew narrower and more windy, set deep between hedgerows of hawthorn and ivy, holly and elder which rustled in a strong wind that seemed to Bianca to have a salty taste, as if it blew from the sea.

'Is it much further? Where is your house?' she asked Matt.

'Not far from the Thames Estuary.'

'The river, not the sea,' she thought aloud.

'What?'

'The wind smells of the sea, but obviously it's the river.'

'It's both. This is a very flat coastline full of little rivers; the Crouch, the Blackwater, the Stour all empty into the sea. Beyond the coast there are great mudflats. At low tide you can walk for hours from Shoeburyness before you find any water. I was born here. In the summer I spent every spare minute fishing, catching crabs, swimming, messing about in boats. I want my daughter to have the happy childhood I had. That was what my wife and I planned—' He broke off; she saw his mouth trembling, his throat moving convulsively as if he was fighting not to cry.

A wave of sympathy filled her. To give him time to recover, she hurriedly said, 'I had the same sort of childhood, but in the West Country, on the Dorset coast. We spent every fine day on the beach; my mother used to despair of keeping my room tidy. I brought home shells, driftwood, seaweed, flowers, pebbles—and arranged them on every possible surface as if they were precious antiques. There's nothing like the sea, is there?'

'Nothing,' he said in a voice roughened by emotion.

'And it's all for free, which is the magic thing about it.'

They slowed to drive through a sleepy village whose shops were all closed. A few teenagers wandered along the street, laughing, before diving into a small eighteenth-century white-painted pub. The pub sign swung to and fro, creaking. It carried a painting of a goat's head, sinister horns, the slanting, ominous yellow eyes staring down at her. Was it meant to be the Devil?

'They do great food,' said Matt. 'And have the sexiest barmaid in Essex.'

She laughed. 'You go there often, I suppose?'

He turned his head to grin at her and she saw he was back to normal, his spasm of emotion over. 'What do you think? Whenever I'm down here I drive over for a drink at The Goat. I ought to come more often. I'm missing out on Lisa's childhood, seeing so little of her; my mother nags me endlessly about it.'

'How old is your mother?' asked Bianca, thinking that Mrs Hearne was very brave, taking on a new baby.

'Sixty-three.'

'Doesn't she find Lisa tiring? Even young mothers find it exhausting to run after three-year-olds.'

He frowned. 'She's never complained.'

'Maybe she didn't want to worry you.' She saw his face tighten, his mouth tense, and wished she had kept her mouth shut. 'Sorry,' she added hurriedly. 'I shouldn't have said anything.' It wasn't her business, anyway, was it?

How thoughtless! As if he hadn't enough to worry about with his mother being rushed off to hospital for an emergency operation. At sixty-three any emergency was likely to have potential dangers. Luckily, an appendectomy was an operation which most surgeons would have frequently performed, but he must be anxious. She could kick herself for saying what she had, implying criticism. She didn't even know his mother. How did she know whether Mrs Hearne was fit enough to take care of a small child?

'You think I've been selfish?' he curtly said, and she bit her lip.

'No, of course not—just...maybe...well, I don't know your mother; she could be having the time of her life, looking after your little girl. Oh, look, I shouldn't have said anything—don't take any notice of me.'

'Huh,' he grunted, lines biting into his forehead. 'Too late to say that. You've put the idea into my head now.'

'I'm sorry,' she guiltily said.

'No, you're right, I have been thoughtless. When my mother's over this I'll talk to her. She has said Lisa should start at playschool in the mornings and that might help. Or maybe I should hire a nanny?'

Bianca didn't risk commenting. She had said more than enough already. She stared out into the dark landscape. The fields on either side were very flat; she saw the occasional cow loom up as they drove past. Bianca thought it dull, compared to the grandeur of the Dorset landscape—the rounded hills, flowing green fields, the ancient hill forts, with their barrows and stone circles, the woods and copses, and the white chalk cliffs along the coast.

They turned a corner and slowed before parking outside a white-painted wooden gate leading into a large garden. By the rising moon Bianca saw the house, half red brick, half timbered, with a black gabled roof of rosy tiles, and a little thicket of trees behind it, to shelter it from the cold, piercing winds blowing in from the estuary and the unseen sea.

Matt switched off the engine and pocketed the ignition key. They both got out and stood staring at the house; a light was on in a downstairs room but otherwise all the windows were dark.

Bianca heard the distant sighing of the sea.

'Tide's changing,' Matt said.

Startled, she asked, 'How can you tell?'

'I can hear it running out—it's quite a different sound when it is coming in.' He turned and looked down at her, his eyes glimmering, mysterious, by moonlight. 'The wind is blowing your hair around your head. It makes you look very different.'

She self-consciously put a hand up to smooth back the loose tendrils of blonde hair, and he pushed her hand down again.

'Leave it. I like it. There's something very sexy about a woman with her hair loose.'

She turned quickly away and pushed open the gate; as it creaked the front door swung wide and a very old woman with a red Paisley shawl around her shoulders hobbled out, leaning on a stick, and peered at them from the doorstep.

'Oh, it's you, Matt. You got here much faster than I expected. I hope you didn't drive too fast.'

She limped towards them, small and frail, her back bowed, her face criss-crossed with lines. If Matt hadn't told her Mrs Morley was eighty Bianca would still have guessed. Age had withered her, shrunk her. Her small black eyes stared from Matt to Bianca and back again, with obvious curiosity, but she discreetly didn't ask any questions.

'Lisa's still asleep in bed. I rang the hospital just now; they said your mother is in the operating theatre. They should have news in an hour or so, if you want to ring then.' She yawned, a trembling, claw-like hand in front of her mouth. 'I'm very tired. This has been quite a shock. I'm fond of your mother; when she rang me tonight she sounded terrible; I hope she's going to be okay.'

'She's very fit, and this is a routine operation; I'm sure she'll soon be better,' Matt said.

The old woman nodded. 'Let's hope so. Well, I'll be off. I left some home-made tomato soup in a pot on the stove. It took my mind off what was happening to do some cooking. There's milk and orange juice in the fridge, some local cheese and half a chicken, too, I noticed, and some of your mother's home-baked bread in the larder. I checked that your room was ready, too.'

'You're very good; I'm very grateful for everything you've done. Get in and I'll drive you home, Mrs Morley; you must be very tired,' Matt said, taking her arm and walking her to the passenger door of his car.

Turning, he said, 'Bianca, why don't you get yourself a drink while you're waiting for me? I won't be long. Mrs Morley lives very close. Just the other end of the lane. You must be hungry. We'll eat as soon as I get back.'

She stood at the open door watching his sports car leap forward, the red fire of the exhaust like a comet behind him as he drove off along the lane to where she glimpsed the dark oblong of a roof behind trees.

The car braked and stopped, Matt got out again, his long black shadow falling over the road in the silvery moonlight. Bianca stared at him for a moment, aware of the deep beating of her heart, a disturbing heat in her body.

What on earth was the matter with her? Why was he having this effect on her?

Angry with herself, she turned hurriedly and went indoors. Standing very still in the black-beamed, white-walled hall, she listened to the sounds of the house, absorbing the atmosphere. A deep-toned clock ticked sonorously somewhere. The old walls creaked. The house was alive, awake.

She loved the look of it—the large stone fireplace, with iron firebacks and a brick lining, the front of it faced with pretty blue-and-white Delft tiles showing men fishing, ladies in long dresses in a garden. A tall dark blue vase stood on the hearth itself, filled with spring flowers—purple lilac, white tulips and a spray of yellow azaleas. The scent of the lilac was heady.

The child was obviously still asleep. There was no sound from upstairs.

Bianca walked through the hall and into the room beyond—a large, modern, comfortable kitchen. The walls were green, the cabinets bright yellow—it would be a good room for mornings; the colours would cheer you up even if it was raining or snowing.

She filled an electric kettle and plugged it in to boil, then reached down two mugs from the hooks on a golden pine dresser which took up most of one wall. Filled with plates and jugs and teapots, it had a cheerful country feel. Who had chosen the china for it—Matt's wife or his mother?

While the kettle was boiling she walked through to the next room, an elegant dining room dominated by a handsome mahogany rectangular table with fine column legs standing on gilded casters.

Bianca admired it from the doorway, glanced over the rest of the furniture in the room, which matched it, looked up at the delicate chandelier in the centre of the ceiling, where plaster roses bloomed in all the corners. This room had a Victorian feel to it. On a long mahogany side table stood a row of silver-framed photographs. Several were wedding photos; she recognised Matt Hearne, and beside him a laughing girl in a full-skirted Victorian wedding dress, a blowing white veil around a radiant face.

Bianca stared at her—what had she been like, this girl who looked so happy? She wasn't beautiful, yet she had a sort of beauty that was a mixture of sweetness and tenderness. Wide, loving eyes, a warm mouth. She would have been easy to like, and to love.

Why didn't Matt Hearne come down here more often? This was a lovely house—if he found the house he had once shared with his wife depressing why didn't he sell it? Was it because he still had not accepted her death?

She turned away, frowning. It took time to get over grief and loss. She knew that.

How long had it been before she began to recover from her mother's death, and before that her father abandoning them both? Pain lingered longer than you ever thought it would.

She heard a footstep and the soft click of the front door closing, and hurried back into the kitchen where the kettle was boiling.

As Matt Hearne appeared she gave him a polite smile. 'Shall I make tea or coffee? And do you want this soup at once?'

'Coffee, please; I'm an addict and I haven't had any

for hours. As to supper, are you happy with just soup and chicken salad?'

'Fine by me.'

'You're a very accommodating guest.'

His ironic tone annoyed her. Her eyes flashed and he laughed.

'Why the glare?'

'Do you have to be so sarcastic?'

His dark brows lifted. 'Was that how it sounded? I didn't intend it that way. I'm really grateful for the way you're taking what's happened. It's an enviable gift, being able to adapt to circumstances.' He gave her his slow, charming smile. She wished she was impervious to it, but she wasn't; her body's response was immediate and infuriating.

'Forgive me?' he murmured, his eyes gleaming.

'I suppose so, although I don't know why I should,' she muttered, turning away to hide the heat in her face, the sudden pulsing in her neck.

Sounding casual, unaware of her reactions, he said, 'Look, if you start heating the soup, I'll just pop up to check on Lisa and make sure she's okay, then I'll come down and make the salad.'

'I can do that.'

'No, I will. Don't worry, I'm not going to leave you to do all the work. You're still my guest.'

'Okay,' she said, bending to turn on the heat under the soup.

He walked behind her and as he did so trailed a fingertip across her nape. She started violently, whirling to face him.

'What do you think you're doing?'

He looked surprised. 'Sorry; I couldn't resist the

temptation. You have a lovely neck. I suddenly wanted to know if it was as smooth as it looked.'

Her green eyes were hostile. 'A man of your age should have learnt to resist that sort of temptation. Keep your hands to yourself, or I'll ring for a taxi, Mr Hearne.'

He backed away, holding his hands in the air. 'Sorry, miss. I'll be good, miss, I promise.'

He went out and she sat down suddenly because her knees were shaking and she felt distinctly weird. It must be exhaustion after a long, draining week, but it felt rather more personal.

She couldn't stay here all night. Not alone, with him. Look at her, trembling like a leaf, when all he had done was touch her with one fingertip! She had offered to stay here and take care of his little girl on impulse because she felt sorry for the child and for him. How could she ever have realised what danger she would be in? Nothing like this had ever happened to her before. She had never had a problem keeping men at bay in the past—but then she had never met a man like Matt Hearne.

The man was a tinderbox, and she was an explosives factory. All he had to do was strike a spark and she would be blown sky-high.

She stared at nothing, trying to stop shaking, trying to stop her heart racing, make her breathing slow down.

If one touch of his finger could cause such havoc, what would happen if he went a lot further?

Thank God Don didn't know what was going on. He had wanted her to engineer just such an intimate situation. He would approve. Bianca did not.

She had to stop thinking. Better to keep busy. She made herself get up again, walked around the kitchen fast, stirring the soup, opening the fridge to look at what it held and getting out the ingredients for a salad.

The soup was ready by the time she heard him coming back, and she had made a bowl of salad. As he walked back into the kitchen Bianca was tossing the ingredients with wooden salad servers, carved heads of angels with spread wings to hold them by. The bowl held cherry tomatoes, slices of cucumber, radishes, a mixture of salad leaves, all coated with a dressing she had made from olive oil, balsamic vinegar, a sprinkling of mustard and a touch of sugar.

'I meant to do that!' Matt said, taking a tomato and eating it. 'Mmm, lovely dressing. You should have left it for me to do, though. I didn't invite you out tonight with the idea of making you into a chef, you know!'

'How could you have guessed what would happen? Let's just make the best of it. Will you bring the chicken to the table?'

'Shall we have it cold or shall I pop it in the microwave?'

'Whatever you like. How was your daughter?'

'Still fast asleep, with her thumb in her mouth. I think she could sleep through an earthquake. I wish I could sleep like that but I've lost the knack of sleeping through the night. Some nights I hardly sleep at all.'

Since his wife's death? she wondered, watching him put the chicken on its wooden platter into the microwave. There were faint shadows on his skin, under those brilliant blue eyes. Was he a one-woman man? Hadn't there been anyone else in the three years since his wife's death?

He was so attractive—a lot of women must have tried to get his attention yet she knew there had never been a whisper of any relationship. Gossip was always an

important part of any assessment of someone whose
company they wanted to acquire. Knowing the weaknesses and strengths of an opponent was essential, and
sex was one obvious key, especially with a man.

She carried the tray set with two bowls of steaming
soup to the table. Matt joined her and picked up his
spoon, bending his head to inhale.

'This smells delicious.'

'Mrs Morley makes very good soup; she obviously
made this with basil, which I love.' She sat down and
shook out the cotton table napkin she had set out beside
the cutlery.

'I love it, too, and I'm starving,' he said, taking a
spoonful of soup.

'So am I,' she admitted, looking at her watch. Her
green eyes widened in surprise. 'And no wonder. It's
nine o'clock!' The evening had gone so fast and so
much had happened. Stirring her soup, she corrected
that—it felt as though so much had happened but in fact
very little actually had, to her, except that their plans
for the evening had been wrecked by his mother's sudden illness.

Oh, come off it! she scolded herself. Hadn't she also
discovered he did something disastrous to her heart rate
merely by being near her?

Even when she was a schoolgirl she couldn't remember reacting to the opposite sex like this! It was ridiculous. She was behaving like a kid with a crush, but
she wasn't a teenager, she was a grown woman.

'Maybe now we can talk some business?' he murmured, and she was startled to remember that that had
been the object of meeting tonight. They were supposed
to be talking about the take-over.

She had to pull herself together! It was time to put

her mind in order, stop these fantasies from taking over the inside of her head.

Huskily, she said, 'The most important point I want to make is that although TTO want to take over your company we want you, yourself, even more. We admire your work, Mr Hearne.'

'Matt.'

'Matt,' she said a little impatiently, because she wanted to get this point over to him, not have him dwelling on unimportant matters like whether she used his first or last name. 'Matt, TTO would value you a great deal. You would have far more money to spend on your research, as much assistance as you need. If you no longer had a company to run you could give free rein to your creativity, Matt.'

'Drink your soup!' was all he said in response.

She frowned, wondering if he was ever going to take her seriously enough to talk through the proposals TTO wanted to make, but obediently concentrated for a few moments on the tomato soup.

'Good, isn't it?' Matt said, and she nodded, putting down her spoon.

He got up to remove their soup bowls and bring over the hot chicken. 'Do you cook, Bianca?'

'I can, but rarely have the time. I tend to buy and microwave food a lot, and salad.'

'Same here. What would you like? Thigh or breast?'

She looked up, frowning. 'What?'

'Chicken,' he said, his mouth twitching. 'Which portion can I give you?'

'You do it deliberately, don't you?' she burst out.

'Do what?'

'Flirt.'

His face was all innocence. 'Was I?'

'You know you were. Will you stop talking to me like that? Either treat me with the same respect you'd show to any other executive or let's stop talking business at all!'

'Does Don Heston treat you with the same respect he shows all his other executives?'

'Yes!'

His brows rose in cold mockery. 'You mean he admires your brains? It isn't just your looks he likes?'

'Yes!' she ground out between her teeth.

He drawled coolly, 'You do know that most people think you're his mistress?'

Yes, she knew; how could she help knowing what some people whispered behind her back? Some of the women in the office deliberately talked loudly enough for it to reach her ears, but if she looked round their faces would be blankly innocent, they would be looking elsewhere, never at her.

Angrily she said, 'I can't help what people think. Especially men like you, who still can't treat women as equals. Did your wife work? Or did you insist she gave up her job after you were married?'

His face darkened. 'Don't drag my wife into this!'

She jumped at the harshness of his voice, the change in his expression.

A silence fell. She put some salad on her plate and began to eat, face averted.

Matt did the same. 'Sorry I snapped,' he muttered without looking at her.

She didn't answer. If he thought he could snarl at her and get away with it with a throw-away pretence of an apology, he was wrong.

'Don't sulk.'

She gave him a cold, level stare. 'I'm not.'

'Smile, and I'll believe you!' He smiled himself, that coaxing, teasing smile loaded with charm.

'You think you're irresistible, don't you?' she drily said, and he laughed, eyes gleaming with amusement.

'Well, aren't I?'

She shook her head. 'No, just deluded.'

But the atmosphere had lightened a good deal, which was just what he had intended. He was devious and manipulative, she thought, finishing her food, but that was hardly a surprise. Weren't most men?

'We'll be more comfortable drinking our coffee in the sitting room,' he said, getting up from the table.

She began to clear the table but he firmly told her to stop. 'I'll deal with that later.'

So she followed him into a pretty room with walls painted a delicate aquamarine, with carpets and curtains a pale gold, making the perfect background to elegant eighteenth-century furniture. She thought the wood was either walnut or rosewood; the chairs, sofa and chaise longue were upholstered in cream velvet, with buttoned backs. If his wife had chosen this furniture, this decor, she must have had wonderful taste. Was that how she had spent her time after marrying Matt? In choosing the furniture and decoration of the house?

A fortune, Bianca thought, staring around—it must all have cost a fortune.

'I'm sorry I snapped,' Matt abruptly said. 'I don't like talking about my wife. I still miss her; it's a painful subject.'

She felt a strange qualm, and was disgusted with herself when she realised she was actually jealous. Oh, for heaven's sake! she thought. How can you be jealous of a dead woman you never even met? Grow up, will you?

Aloud she muttered, 'Don't worry about it, I understand. Tell me how you came to found your company?'

'I worked for other firms for years before I started my own. That's why I know the sort of restrictions companies place on their employees. I promised myself that I would never be in the power of other people again, never be forced to work on projects that I hadn't originated. Whatever your people say now they'd change their tune once they got me signed up. They would start ordering me to do this or that, rather than allowing me to follow my own instincts.'

Earnestly, she insisted, 'Believe me, Matt, they wouldn't; I know Don himself is very keen indeed on your current project, the voice-activated computer.'

He gave her a wry look. 'And if I try to work on some other project?'

She was taken aback. 'Well, I...but surely...you would want to finish work on such an exciting project first?'

'Sometimes I break off work on one idea to work on something else. I'm not a robot. My mind gets to the end of one seam of an idea, and I break off for a while—maybe for weeks, if not months—to do something else. The change is refreshing, gives me a new lease on life.'

She looked down, frowning, not knowing what to say. He was right. Don would be furious if he stopped work on the major project, for any reason, and would try to coerce him into going back to it at once. Her eye fell on her watch and she suddenly remembered Mrs Hearne.

'You were going to ring the hospital,' she reminded him, and he looked at the delicate French clock on the mantelpiece, finished his coffee and got up.

'Yes, she must be out of the operating theatre by now.'

While he made his call Bianca carried the coffee tray back to the kitchen and started clearing the table. She was loading the dish-washer when he came back. Looking round anxiously, she asked him, 'Is she okay?'

He looked quite calm, anyway. He was half-smiling, and there was no distress in his eyes. 'They said she had taken the operation well and there were no problems, so far. She's a tough old lady. I think she'll soon be home. At least I can visit her tomorrow and then I'll be able to see for myself how she is.' He looked around the tidy kitchen. ''You shouldn't have done all this—I told you I was going to do it. I'm house-trained, I live alone and take care of myself. You're looking tired; I think we've talked enough business for one evening. Well, I know I have. I'll just put this machine on then I'll show you to your bedroom.'

That was when Bianca began to get very nervous, facing the fact that she was here in this house, alone with him, except for a small child, for the night.

A disturbing thought popped into her head. Flushing, she stammered, 'I...j-just r-realised—I haven't got...I suppose you couldn't lend me...something to wear in bed?' Normally she wouldn't mind sleeping naked, or in her slip, but not with him a door or two away.

What if his little girl cried in the night? How could she go and comfort her if she had nothing to wear?

He didn't look either amused or embarrassed. Calmly, he nodded. 'Of course; I'll find you a pair of my pyjamas.' His blue eyes measured her thoughtfully. 'My mother wears flannelette nighties; I don't think you'd like them and they would be like tents on you. My pyjamas would be better. I'm taller, and not as thin as you are, so they'll be big on you, too, but they'll do for one night.'

When they reached the top of the stairs the house was so quiet that Bianca clearly heard the gentle, rhythmic breathing of the sleeping child from her own small room and felt a strong curiosity. She wished she could see her, but it might wake her up.

Matt opened a door into a square, chintzy room next door. 'Will this room do?'

She looked around. 'It's very pretty and looks quite comfortable.'

'Good. I'll find the pyjamas for you.' He walked away along the landing to another door and she followed him into a large, elegant room with an enormous Victorian brass bed in the centre of it. Dark red velvet curtains hung at the windows, a dark red-and-black patterned carpet on the floor, and the bed was draped with a cream broderie anglaise duvet and piles of matching pillows. A fitted wardrobe ran along one wall, floral china knobs on each door.

A shiver rippled down her back. So, this was the bedroom he had shared with his wife. That was the bed in which they had slept together. On the bedside table she saw a silver-framed photograph of the dark-haired, smiling girl she had seen in those wedding photos downstairs. Every night Matt went to bed with her face next to his pillow. Reminding him of their love, keeping his grief alive.

How would he ever get over her?

She caught herself up. Why should she care about that? If he wanted to spend the rest of his life in mourning for a dead woman it was no business of hers.

But three years of grief was far too long. Human beings had to live in the present, not the past.

Matt came back with a pair of navy silk pyjamas which he handed to her. 'Here you are. You could probably get away with just wearing the top; it's quite long.' He looked down at her legs. 'I guess it would come halfway down your thighs, anyway.'

She muttered, 'Thanks,' and walked out carrying the pyjamas. She had a physical awareness of him that was growing worse by the minute. Every time he looked at her it felt as if he was touching her.

Or was that only what she wanted? To have him touch her?

'Anything else you need?' he asked from behind her, and her breathing quickened.

'No, thank you.' Of course he had meant the question in a straightforward way. It was just her hyper-charged imagination that had invested it with disturbing echoes. She was getting paranoid; seeing implications that were not there. It must be because she was tired, and because Don had put the idea of seduction into her head before she ever met Matt Hearne. If Don had never suggested she should lead him on she wouldn't be so jumpy now.

'A glass of water in case you get thirsty later?'

'Oh. Yes, please.' The last thing she wanted to do was wander around the house tonight wearing only his pyjama top to get some water.

'I'll bring one up.'

'Thank you.' She couldn't risk looking at him in case he caught a glimpse of the turmoil inside her.

He went back downstairs and she went into the bedroom he had allocated to her. There was a lock on the door, to her relief, and she had a pretty, but rather small bathroom. She turned down the bed, closed the curtains, while she waited for Matt to return.

He tapped on the door and she opened it. Handing

her a glass of water, he said, 'Goodnight, and thank you
for offering to help out. If Lisa wakes up in the night
I'll deal with her, don't worry. I'm afraid she wakes up
pretty early in the morning but you don't have to get
up until you're ready. I can cope with dressing her, and
making her breakfast. But I have some international
calls to make later in the morning—do you think you
could look after her for a few hours while I'm working?'

'Of course; I'd enjoy it.'

He smiled. 'Thank you. I hope you sleep well.'

He walked away and she closed the door and locked
it as quietly as possible before going into the bathroom.
When she had washed off her make-up and brushed her
blonde hair for the night she put on the pyjama top and
studied her reflection in the mirror.

Sliding into the bed, she switched off the lamp on
her bedside table. Moonlight trickled over the walls like
water. Bianca lay staring at it for what seemed hours,
thinking about Matt.

She woke up suddenly, eyes flying open, and for a
second couldn't remember where she was or why. Then
she realised a child was crying somewhere, a soft, plain-
tive sound.

'Grandma...Grandma...'

Bianca's memory came back in a rush; she pushed
back the bedclothes and slid out of bed, hurried into the
room next door. Lisa was sitting up in bed, staring as
the door opened.

Hearing the gasp of shock and alarm the child gave
as she saw someone she did not know, Bianca hurriedly
switched on the light so that Lisa could see her properly
and went over to sit on the edge of the child's bed.

She was smaller than Bianca had expected—a tiny,

finely featured child, with blue eyes like her father and
dark hair cut in a neat bob around her face.

She shrank in the bed, staring.

'Don't be scared!' Bianca said softly. 'I'm a friend
of your daddy; I'm staying here just for tonight. I heard
you call out.'

'Grandma,' Lisa whispered. 'I want Grandma.'

'Grandma isn't here at the moment. She'll be back
soon, don't worry. What did you want? Is something
wrong? Or did you just wake up and feel lonely?'
Bianca stroked the girl's soft hair. 'My name is Bianca.
I know your name; it's Lisa, isn't it?'

'Go away,' the child said, tears trembling on her
thick, dark lashes. 'Don't like you; go away.'

'I like you. What pretty pyjamas; you look lovely in
them.'

Distracted slightly, Lisa looked down at the white
cotton pyjamas printed with a variety of teddy bears.
Her tears stopped and her pink bow mouth took on a
satisfied curve.

'Teddies,' she said. 'All over. I chose them.'

'Did you? That was a good choice. I like teddies, too;
I have a very old teddy bear who sits on my bed all the
time.'

Lisa looked surprised, staring at her.

'What's his name?'

'Edgar. I was given him when I was little, by my
father.'

A sting of shock went through her as she said that.
She had almost forgotten how she got her bear.

Until now.

How strange that she should remember that moment
suddenly. The memory was so strong, as if it had happened only the other day. Her father bending down to

pick her up, lifting her on to his knee, kissing her, and showing her a bear dressed in a sailor suit, with a white cap on his furry head.

'Happy birthday, baby. He's for you—do you like him? You'll look after him, won't you?'

And she had. For so many years he had been all she had to remind her of her father, whose name had never been mentioned since he left. Her mother had thrown out all the photos of him, all his clothes and books. Suddenly her father had no longer existed for them. Her mother had been very bitter; hate had burned deep inside her, and Bianca sometimes felt that hate had created the cancer her mother died from.

Hating was dangerous, destructive, ate its way into your flesh and mind.

'My daddy gived me a kangaroo.' Lisa pointed. 'Kanga, I call her.'

The large brown fur animal stood on the windowsill behind the bed.

'How lovely,' Bianca said huskily, hoping Lisa would never be in her position, never find herself without a father and only this stuffed toy to remember him by.

Tears welled up in the child's eyes again. 'My daddy. Want my daddy.'

Hurriedly, Bianca asked, 'Shall I wake your daddy? He's asleep in his room.'

'Yes, want Daddy,' Lisa sobbed. 'Want him, now.'

Bianca got up and turned to the door only to see Matt leaning there, wearing a dark red silk dressing gown over matching pyjamas.

How long had he been there?

'Here is your daddy,' she told the child, who beamed, holding out her arms. Matt walked past Bianca and

picked up his daughter, lifting her out of bed and holding her tightly, kissing her on the top of her head, on
her pale, tear-stained cheek.

'Hello, darling—what's the matter?'

Bianca went back to her own room. For some reason
it hurt to see them together, the child and her father.
They did not need her now. They only needed each
other.

Matt Hearne might be wealthy and successful but that
didn't heal his heartbreak or make his relationship with
his child any easier. How could he have left her here
while he lived most of his life in London? How did
Lisa feel about that? Why was human life so compli-
cated?

She got back into bed but didn't put out the light; sat
there, her knees up and her chin resting on them, staring
at nothing, and thinking about her father, Matt Hearne,
Don Heston—men in general, the way they ran their
lives and treated their women and children.

This was still a man's world. Women might get good
jobs these days; they might live more independent and
successful lives. But where men were concerned they
were still second-class citizens.

Time passed. She grew cold and was about to lie
down and put out the light when there was a tap on her
door.

'Yes?' she called, defensively stiffening.

He opened the door. 'She's asleep again.'

She was intensely on edge, sitting up in bed with him
a few feet away, staring at her.

'Thanks for taking care of her until I got there.'

She gestured the thanks away. 'That's okay. She's
very sweet.'

He smiled. 'I'm sorry she woke you. Look, I'm going

to make myself some hot chocolate—can I get some for you?'

She nodded. 'Thanks. I'd love some.'

'No problem. I won't be a minute.'

He vanished again and she leapt out of the bed to look at herself anxiously in the dressing-table mirror.

As she had been afraid, her blonde hair was loose and tousled, her face flushed, and the silk pyjama top clung to her warm body, outlining her breasts, her slim waist. Below the hem of it you could clearly see her thighs and long, bare legs. No wonder she had felt him staring.

She began brushing her hair only to freeze at the sound of a bell downstairs. The telephone? Who on earth would ring at this hour? The hospital? It had to be bad news about his mother. Poor Matt.

Then she realised it wasn't the phone—there was someone at the front door. Startled, Bianca picked up her watch from the dressing table.

It was gone midnight. Who on earth would come here at this time of night?

Footsteps hurried along the hall, she heard the front door being unbolted, opened, then low voices murmuring—she easily picked out Matt's voice, but the other sounded like a woman.

Bianca tiptoed out on to the landing and peered down the stairs. A woman in a close-fitting cream jersey suit stood just inside the front door, very close to Matt Hearne.

'I had to come...' she was saying

Matt put his arm around her and bent his head to kiss her.

Bianca watched in shock and disbelief.

It was Sara Heston.

CHAPTER FOUR

BIANCA was so shaken that she tiptoed back to her bedroom and climbed into bed. What was Don's wife doing here at this time of night? Their home was nowhere near here.

How often did she come here at weekends when Matt was here? Or had he rung to tell her his mother was in hospital, but forgotten to mention that he wasn't alone in the house, and was this a perfectly innocent, one-off visit?

Oh, come on, she thought—in the middle of the night?

'I had to come...' Sara Heston had said to him, and flung her arms round him. He had kissed her.

Bianca shut her eyes, but she could still see them, in her mind's eye, his silky brown head bending, her face lifted up for his kiss. Intimate, familiar, hardly the way acquaintances of the opposite sex behaved. After all, the way Matt had spoken about her, you would have assumed they barely knew each other!

What had he said exactly? Just that Sara had been at school with his wife and he had met her only recently.

Do I believe that? she asked herself, and knew she didn't. What was the truth? Were they lovers?

With Don in the middle of a take-over bid that was worrying. How would he feel if he found out his wife was secretly involved with the man whose firm he had targeted? How much did Sara Heston know about her husband's business?

Not much, probably. Living in the country and rarely coming to London, she was unlikely to be aware of the day-to-day running of the company. Did Don talk to her about business when he did go home? It was possible, but not probable, which must mean that his wife couldn't betray him.

But would she? If she had the chance?

Bianca didn't know her well enough to guess, but all her feminine instincts screamed out that she had just discovered a disturbing situation.

Should she tell Don?

There had always been gossip about Don and other women. Quite apart from the whispering about herself, Bianca could remember having heard talk about Don from way back, when she'd first joined the firm. Don was not the faithful type and seemed to have lived a separate life from his wife and children for years.

Sara Heston must have heard talk, too, surely? Some 'friend' would have enjoyed telling her, pretending sympathy, concern, when in fact they just wanted to make sure she knew what her husband was up to.

Maybe she had deliberately started to see Matt just to punish Don, to get her own back?

Bianca could see Sara's point of view; she knew she would have been angry if she were in Sara's situation. Any woman would. The pain and humiliation must be unbearable. Bianca sympathised with her. Or she would do, except that...

She put her hands over her face, pressing in on her cheekbones, her eye sockets, as if trying to expunge the memory of what she had seen.

Except that Sara had picked on Matt.

She reddened angrily at that admission, her face turning hot under her hands.

No, that wasn't it; it wasn't her business what he did, or with whom.

A second later she heard footsteps outside, then a tap on her door.

She swallowed, snatching her hands down, trying to breathe calmly, to look normal.

'Come in!' Even to her own ears her voice sounded husky and she flinched as he came into the room.

He shot her a quick look, frowning. 'Something wrong?'

'You just made me jump, that's all.'

His blue eyes were hard and narrow, observing her as if he was angry. 'I told you I'd bring you some hot chocolate. There's no need to act as if you thought I was Genghis Khan!' He strode over to the bed and put a bright pink porcelain mug down on the bedside table.

'Thank you.' Bianca couldn't stop staring at his long, supple, sinewy hands. They had just been touching Don's wife. Had the two of them been talking downstairs, or making love?

She wished she could shut such disturbing thoughts out of her head. Why did she keep thinking about it? It was nothing to do with her what they did.

Matt's eyes roamed over her in a leisurely exploration. 'My pyjama top never looked that good on me. And I love your hair loose; much better than the buttoned-up Victorian look you usually go in for.'

'I always wear my hair like that at work.' She was speaking automatically, her mind busy on something very different. How long would Sara be staying? Had she come intending to spend the night with Matt?

'Keeps the men at bay, does it?' His mouth twisted, cynicism in his eyes.

Under his gaze her body was rigid against the sensuous silk of his pyjama top, her nipples hard, her breasts swelling, full and high. She didn't want him looking at her like that, especially when she knew he had another woman downstairs, waiting for him, yet she could not control the instinctive responses of her body. It was as if they led separate lives, her brain and her body. Their reactions to him were miles apart. Her head told her she could not trust him, did not like him.

'Is it you who doesn't like male attention—or is it Don Heston who objects?'

The sharp, stinging question was a shock; she shrank back from him, breathing raggedly. Although she didn't know why she should be so shaken. He had already accused her, to her face, of being Don's mistress, hadn't he? She knew now who had given him that impression. Don's wife. Bianca felt sick at the thought of what Sara must have said about her. She couldn't get a word out in self-defence; it was too humiliating to talk about.

He waited for her to answer, and when she was silent drawled, 'So it is true? Well, drink your hot chocolate and get some sleep. You must be very tired. Goodnight.'

She hated the contempt in his eyes, the ice in his tone. What right had he to stand in judgement on her? He was having an affair with Don's wife, yet he sneered at what he thought was going on between her and Don. That double-standard didn't surprise her—all men seemed to operate two standards—but it made her very angry.

How dared he?

Of course, he didn't know she had seen Sara; he had no idea she knew Don's wife was in the house, or that she had guessed about their affair. That was his little secret—his and Sara's! But he felt justified in talking to her in a voice loaded with distaste.

She watched him walk back to the door, a very tall man who managed to dominate this little room without even trying. He had a physical presence which rippled through her like the after-shocks of an earthquake. Nothing in her life would ever be the same after today. Her world had been blown apart and the landscape would be unrecognisable from now on.

She watched the door close, heard him running downstairs. Running to her. To Sara Heston.

He couldn't wait to get back to Don's wife.

Jealousy stung like the bite of a snake, but she had no right to feel this way. He didn't belong to her. She had only known the man a couple of days. She was nothing to him, either, except a chance acquaintance he obviously disliked, was hostile to, because she was part of a predatory company trying to take his firm away from him, and because he thought she was Don's mistress, and Matt was in love with Don's wife.

The whole situation was like a knot of serpents, twisted and poisonous.

She looked at her watch again—the night was seeping away, minute by minute. She ought to get some sleep; she was going to feel like death in the morning; she was very tired and yet wide awake.

Picking up the pink mug, she sipped the thick, creamy chocolate without even noticing what she was drinking, staring at nothing and shivering in spite of the warm bedclothes covering her.

What did she do now? Did she tell Don?

She felt feverish, yet chilled, distracted, unable to think straight. Her body kept jangling like a peal of bells every time Matt came into her head.

Pull yourself together! she thought, putting down the empty mug and diving down under the bedclothes. You're only here because Don asked you to have dinner with Matt Hearne. This was not personal, it was business. How many times in the past had she had private talks with men whose companies they were acquiring? Nothing like this had ever happened before.

Why was this time so different?

Well, for a start, this time Don's wife was downstairs…doing what? Betraying Don, in some way or another, whether emotionally or physically—what other explanation could there be?

Yes, she was going to have to tell Don. He would be furious if he ever found out his wife had been here, secretly, and Bianca had known but hadn't told him. He would see it as betrayal on her part; he expected her to keep him fully informed of every piece in the complex jigsaw of a take-over bid.

Yet how could she?

She lay in the dark, listening, but hearing nothing, not even a low murmur of voices. Maybe Sara had gone?

Bianca silently slid out of bed and crept to the window, drew back the edge of the curtain and peered out. There was Matt's car. And parked behind it another one—a dark saloon, long, sleek, expensive, glossy. That had to be Sara's car. She was obviously still here.

What were they doing? Waiting for her to go to sleep? And then what? Would they creep up to his room to sleep together in Matt's bed? Or would they make love downstairs?

She felt sick. On the carpet, on a couch…their bodies naked, pale and gleaming, twisting together in passion. Disturbing images filled her head, made her shudder.

She listened to the ticking clock, hearing nothing else, suspecting everything. It must have been gone two when she finally drifted off into an uneasy doze.

She woke abruptly in daylight to hear the child chattering and Matt's deep voice answering her as he carried her down the stairs.

Bianca shot out of bed to look out of the window. Sara Heston's car had gone. She looked at her watch—it was only eight o'clock! How much sleep had she had? Five, six hours? Not enough. She felt terrible, her head pounding, eyes aching.

But she had to get up; she couldn't go back to sleep, as she normally did on a Saturday or Sunday morning, catching up on all the sleep she had not got during the week. She hurriedly showered and got dressed, did her hair in the usual way, put on make-up, yawning all the time. As she went downstairs to join the other two she heard Lisa still chattering.

'Not cornflakes, Daddy, no! Pollidge…pollidge, please, Daddy.'

Matt sounded as weary as Bianca felt—had he been awake for hours last night, making love to Sara Heston? He deserved to be exhausted. She hoped he felt like hell.

'I'm not sure how you cook it, darling. Wait; it tells you how to do it on the box.'

He looked round as he heard Bianca, a large cereal box held in his hand. This morning he was clean-shaven, his pale brown, silky hair brushed smoothly, and he was wearing a crisp blue shirt, pale blue jeans, a narrow black leather belt around his waist. He looked very sexy; Bianca's heart distinctly missed a beat.

The little girl stared at her, eyes rounding, mouth opening.

'I dreamed you. Last night. I dreamed you.'

Bianca bent to kiss her on the top of her head. 'No, it wasn't a dream, Lisa. I'm real. I did come to see you in bed last night. My name is Bianca; remember me telling you that?'

'Bee,' Lisa said, and giggled. 'Bzzz...buzzy bee.'

'That's what my friends at school all called me,' Bianca said, laughing. 'You can call me Bee, if you like.'

'Do you sting people?' Matt asked, and she gave him a cool, dismissive stare.

'Only if they annoy me.'

'And I do?' he mockingly enquired.

'Bzzz...bzzz...' Lisa hummed. 'Pollidge, Daddy, make pollidge.'

Matt sighed. 'Okay, I'm going to have a shot.'

'I'll do it,' Bianca told him. 'Do you want some, too, or is it just for me and Lisa?'

He handed her the cereal box with relief. 'Thanks. Yes, I'll have some; I haven't eaten porridge for years. In fact, I rarely eat breakfast, and if I do it is usually toast. Coffee or tea for you?'

'Coffee, please.'

He began to make coffee, asking over his shoulder, 'What do you want to drink, angel? Orange juice?'

Lisa nodded, watching Bianca get a large pudding basin down from one of the kitchen cupboards, take a mug and measure oats into the basin, then add the right amount of water.

'Grandma makes pollidge in a pan,' Lisa disapprovingly told her.

Bianca smiled at her. 'That's one way of making it— or you can do it this way—it will taste just the same.'

She put the basin in the microwave, tapped the buttons, and the oven began to turn busily, whirring, while the child stared fixedly at it.

'It go round and round and round.'

'That's right, it's cooking, but you must never touch it; it would burn you. Would you like some fruit, Lisa?'

She had noticed a china bowl of fruit displayed on the kitchen counter. Lisa turned to look at it, nodding.

'Nana, please.'

Bianca peeled a banana and chopped it into slices on a small plate which she put in front of Lisa, who popped a piece into her mouth, mumbling 'Thank you' through the banana.

She was well brought up but there was a primness about her that was unusual in so young a child; all the result, of course, of being brought up by her grandmother. This house was so isolated. Did she ever play with other children? Or was she alone with her grandmother day after day?

The microwave pinged but Bianca left the porridge to stand for a couple of minutes as it was far too hot to eat yet. Matt had poured the coffee and was sitting down at the kitchen table eating an orange he had peeled and sliced. Bianca ate an apple before she put the porridge into bowls. She poured milk on to Lisa's, spooned sugar on to the top, and put it in front of the child.

'Bears,' Lisa said, smiling suddenly and showing pearly white teeth.

Placing his bowl of porridge in front of Matt and putting her own down on the table, too, Bianca had to think twice about what the child had said, then she laughed.

'Yes, bears like porridge—do you know the story of the three bears and Goldilocks, Lisa?'

Lisa nodded. 'Tell me again. I like it.'

While they ate Bianca told the story in ritual fashion, as she had learnt it herself as a child, and Lisa joined in now and then.

'"Who's been sitting on my chair?" said the Daddy Bear!'

She waved her porridgey spoon about while she glee-fully shouted the words and Matt ducked as porridge flew past his ear.

'Hey, watch it!'

The phone began to ring. Matt leapt up as if having expected it. He didn't take the call in the kitchen, al-though there was an extension on the wall, but vanished into another room.

Was it Sara ringing him? To stop herself thinking about that Bianca kept busy, clearing the table, washing up, tidying the room, then took Lisa off to wash her hands and face which were sticky with porridge.

'Want to go out,' Lisa demanded. 'Play in garden.'

Looking out of the window, Bianca saw it was a bright spring morning, so she dressed the child in a green anorak and yellow boots which Lisa showed her in her wardrobe. They made the little girl look like a pixie.

Matt appeared in the hall as they got back downstairs. 'I'm sorry; that was an urgent business call. I have to make some other calls now—could you keep an eye on Lisa until I've finished? I'll try not to take too long.'

'That's okay. I'll take her for a walk if you can lend me some boots.'

He frowned. 'Boots? I don't think…'

'In the back porch,' suggested Lisa. 'In the cupboard, green boots.'

Bianca picked up reluctance in Matt, but Lisa had

already run to the back of the house, leaving them to follow. They found her in a porch adjoining the kitchen. She was opening a cupboard running round the porch, topped with a window seat with dark blue cushions.

Lisa pulled out knee-high dark green boots triumphantly. Bianca glanced uncertainly at Matt and found his face pale, tense.

Then she understood. These were his wife's boots, left here, forgotten, all this time. Did the child know they had once been her dead mother's?

Lisa held them out to her, beaming. She was pleased with herself, and obviously had no idea whose boots she held.

Bianca gave Matt a veiled, hesitant look. What should she do? She could see he was upset. He would probably hate to see her wearing things that had belonged to his wife.

But he had himself under control. 'Yes, please borrow them,' he said politely, his expression blank. 'I'd forgotten them.' He pulled down a wax jacket from a hook in the porch. 'You'd better wear this, too. It can be quite windy near the river.'

Bianca did not want to, but she couldn't think of an excuse for refusing. She put on the jacket, sat down on the window seat and gingerly slid her feet into the boots, half hoping they would be too small—but they fitted perfectly.

'Are they comfortable?' Matt asked, and she nodded without looking at him.

'Yes, thank you. Let's go, Lisa.' Taking the child's hand, she led her back through the house to the front door. 'Which would be the best way to walk?' she asked Matt.

'Turn right and walk through the field at the end of

the lane. That leads down to the estuary. You'll see lots of birds if you go that way, but it will be very muddy.' He sounded casual, cheerful.

He stood, waving, the wind winnowing his soft brown hair, making the blue shirt ripple over the powerful muscles of his chest. They set off along the lane at Lisa's pace and when they looked round again the door had shut.

'Daddy gone,' Lisa said glumly, her mouth turning down at the corners.

'Daddy's busy, but he'll be waiting for us when we get back,' Bianca reassured her, and the little girl cheered up.

Lowering her voice to a confidential murmur, she told Bianca, 'Daddy busy. Always busy. He lives in London because he's too busy to live with me and Grandma.'

It was only too clear that she wished her father lived with her. Little girls always adored their fathers and longed to be with them all the time. Bianca could remember how much she had loved her own father, and how much it had hurt when he went away.

'But Daddy loves you a lot,' Bianca assured her, stroking the child's wind-blown dark hair, and Lisa looked up, those pearly little teeth showing in one of the smiles that was so like her father's.

They reached the end of the lane and went over a stile into the field beyond, met by a fresh, salty wind that tossed their hair about and blew into their faces. It was good walking weather. The field had been ploughed lately; they had to walk around it, following a head-high hedge.

The land was so flat, fields a patchwork of green and brown, with here and there the silver gleam of water mirroring the sky, which seemed to stretch on to eternity—a vivid blue, but with a feathering of white clouds blowing and billowing on the wind's height.

Lisa stumped along, stopping every so often to pick wildflowers from the depths of the hedge—the enamelled yellow of buttercups, creamy primroses, spears of dark bluebells, pink-eyed white daisies. Before long she had an untidy bunch of flowers clutched in one hand. In sniffing them she had also acquired a smudge of yellow pollen on her nose. Bianca smiled every time she saw it.

They came out on a muddy river bank looking out over the gleaming estuary where gulls and waders fed at the tidal edge, their long bills poking and prying into the mud to search for worms, insects and shellfish. Bianca recognised great flocks of plovers with pink legs, curlews, snipe and sandpipers, zigzagging up into nervous flight as the two humans appeared.

Excitedly Lisa ran towards them. Bianca hurried after her, calling out, 'Wait for me!'

Bianca ran too fast. A second later her feet skidded under her and she felt herself slide out of control. Arms flailing, she toppled sideways, down the steep bank, into the low, muddy water, giving a wild yell of alarm.

She landed with a squelchy thump, face down in the mud, so winded for a minute that she couldn't move or think.

The next thing she saw was Lisa's yellow boots, the feet now thickly coated with mud.

'Are you okay, Bee?' the child anxiously asked.

Bianca groaned, clambering up. 'I think so.'

Lisa began giggling. 'You're all muddy. All over.'

'I know.' There wasn't just mud on her face and hands but right down the front of her clothes—she could taste it in her mouth; it caked her nose and eyes. She looked around desperately for clean water, but the tide was too far out; she could only see muddy pools and a seepage of low water oozing over the river bottom. Suddenly, though, she caught sight of a trickle of clear water coming down the bank. That must be a small stream entering the river. Helplessly she plodded over there and held her hands under the cascade; when they were clean she began to wash her face carefully, cleaning her eyes, nose and mouth.

Lisa was splashing cheerfully about, picking up shells, one hand still clutching her wild flowers, running after sea birds who flew up and scattered at her approach.

'I think we'd better go back now,' Bianca called, and the child reluctantly joined her.

They made their way around the field again, even slower this time, because Bianca's boots were clogged by mud; she kept getting stuck in a rut and having to pull herself out before she could go on.

The front door opened before they reached it. Matt stared incredulously at Bianca, his gaze roving from her mud-caked hair to her feet.

'My God, what on earth have you been doing? Swimming in the river while the tide was out?'

Furious, close to tears, she muttered, 'I fell over.'

He considered her, brows rising. 'You should see yourself!'

She was glad she couldn't. Lisa giggled with delight, sitting down on the front doorstep to take off her boots, then running indoors to shed her coat.

'You had better take those boots off, too,' Matt told Bianca. 'My mother will blow her top if that mud gets trodden through the house.'

She leaned on the door frame to kick the first boot

off, but her foot refused to come out of it for a few seconds. When it came at last it did so with a loud squelch, revealing that her foot was as muddy as the outside of the boot.

Tears welled in Bianca's eyes. 'I'm sorry; mud has got inside; I've ruined the boots,' she whispered. He was going to hate her for destroying something that had belonged to his dead wife.

'Never mind; I was going to get rid of them, anyway,' he said coolly, kneeling to take the other boot off.

He stood up again and a second later had bent to pick Bianca up bodily.

'What are you doing?' she gasped, clutching at him, dizzy as her feet left the ground and she found herself held against his chest.

'I'm going to carry you upstairs to the bathroom. You can't walk about with all that mud on your feet but you badly need a hot shower and clean clothes. Come on, Lisa, you go first.'

'I haven't got any clean clothes!'

Lisa was scrambling up the stairs in front of them. 'Bee fell in mud,' she boasted. 'Bee all dirty. Me not muddy.'

'You're quite muddy enough,' her father informed her, carrying Bianca into the bathroom *en suite* with her bedroom. He dumped her unceremoniously into the bath then moved a linen basket from the corner of the room so that it stood next to the bath.

Calmly he ordered, 'Get those clothes off, drop them in the basket then have a shower. There's a towelling robe hanging behind the door. When you're clean and dry, put the robe on, and bring the linen basket downstairs so that your clothes can go into the washing machine.'

He shut the door before she could come up with an answer. Bianca heard him saying to his little girl, 'Now, let's get you cleaned up, Lisa.'

For a moment or so Bianca just stood there feeling ridiculous and furious all at the same time. Who did he think he was? How dared he order her around in that high-handed way? Was that how he ran his company? But there was no point in refusing to obey. She could hardly go on wearing these muddy clothes.

Leaning over, she bolted the bathroom door, then crossly began stripping off everything she was wearing, dropping each item into the open linen basket.

The long, warm shower was heavenly. She used a lot of shower gel to get rid of the smell of mud and salt on her body, before she washed her hair in matching shampoo, then rinsed herself, almost groaning at the wonderful sensation of finally being clean and smelling good.

Slicking back her long, wet hair, after wringing it out, she reached for the white towelling robe and stepped out of the bath.

When she had dried herself thoroughly she unbolted the door and opened it. She couldn't hear Matt or Lisa anywhere. They must be somewhere downstairs. Barefoot, she carried the linen basket down to the kitchen, where she found the other two.

Lisa with a flushed, clean face, wearing a bright blue cotton T-shirt and leggings now sat at the table colouring in a book while Matt had the fridge door open and was glancing through the contents. They both looked round. Lisa cheerfully approved, 'Bee all clean now. Me all clean, too.'

Matt did not say anything, but his vivid eyes explored Bianca in the damp, clinging robe, from the open lapels which just covered the rise and fall of her high breasts, down over her tightly belted waist to the long, bare legs beneath the short hemline of the robe.

She tried not to react to that stare but felt heat kindling in her face and throat.

Huskily, she muttered, 'I'll put my clothes in the washing machine, shall I?'

'Go ahead. Would you like some coffee?'

'Thank you, I'd love some.'

She began pushing her clothes into the washing machine, used the box of soap powder Matt handed her, selected a programme and turned the controls to start the wash. He stood there watching her, too close for comfort, very male in his jeans and shirt, the scent of his body making her skin prickle with edgy awareness.

Lisa slid down to the floor. 'Watch cartoons now,' she informed her father.

Matt looked undecided. 'Does Grandma let you watch them?'

Lisa nodded vigorously.

'Well, show me what sort of cartoons they are,' Matt told her, picking her up as if she was a doll. Was that where he had acquired the habit of forcibly carrying people around in spite of their lack of enthusiasm for the pastime? He was so used to getting his own way with his child that he operated in the same way with adults, given half a chance.

'Bee take me.' Lisa wriggled to get down, kicking her short, fat legs, but Matt just smiled as if her protests amused him. In much the same way that he had merely smiled at Bianca when she tried to argue with him.

'Bianca is going to drink her coffee, you'll see her again later.'

When they had left the room Bianca sat down, picking up the book in which Lisa had been colouring, smiling at the vivid crayons used. Children always loved bright colours. Lisa hadn't managed to keep within the lines, not that that mattered.

She sipped the strong, black coffee Matt had made, then jumped as the telephone began to ring. She expected Matt to answer it but it went on ringing. Was he ignoring it, or was there no extension in whichever room he and Lisa were in?

At last she got up and answered it. 'Hello?'

A silence at the other end, then Don Heston's voice asked, 'Bianca? Is that you?'

She felt as if her stomach had dropped out of her.

'Yes, hello, Don,' she whispered.

'I don't believe this,' he said flatly. 'I've been ringing you at home all morning. Then I tried ringing Hearne's London flat, and got no reply there, either. As a long shot, I rang this number, in case he had gone into the country for the weekend. I thought he might know where you were.'

'Are you ringing me from the plane? I thought you weren't allowed to use mobiles during a flight?'

Don did not seem to be listening to her. He sounded dazed, incredulous. 'My God, I didn't believe you would, but you did, didn't you? I know I suggested you might seduce him into seeing things our way, but I never expected...' He broke off and audibly swallowed, then said hoarsely, 'I can't talk any more. I'll ring again when I can think straight.'

The phone went dead. She replaced it, trembling, icy with shock. Behind her she heard a movement and looked round, wide-eyed, pale.

Matt stared at her across the room, his expression hard; eyes narrowed, jawline tense.

'I thought Heston had gone to Australia?'

'How do you know it was Don? Were you listening in somewhere?' She was horrified by the idea that he had heard Don's accusation, that he knew Don suspected they had slept together. Now he would realise that Don had suggested she seduce him, and he would despise her even more than he already did.

He frowned, his mouth twisting angrily. 'I wasn't eavesdropping, I simply walked in just now and heard you use his name! What was he saying to you? Did he hang up on you? Why? What's going on, Bianca?'

CHAPTER FIVE

SHE didn't answer, couldn't answer, staring back at him, her skin pale, her body tense. She couldn't tell him what Don had said; she didn't want him to know what Don thought. The memory of Don's suggestion that she seduce Matt was a bruise on her mind. She wished she could forget about it, but it kept aching again.

Matt waited, watching her with those hard, narrowed eyes, which kept wandering downwards from her agitated face to the warm curves of her body in the short towelling robe. He despised her, and it showed. Bianca hated knowing how he felt about it. Even though she knew she was innocent, it still hurt.

Abruptly, he asked, 'Have you been ringing him when I wasn't around? I haven't seen you using the phone.'

'I didn't!'

'So how did he know you were here?'

The sharp question made her draw breath, seeing the trap he had laid for her. Yes, obviously—why would Don ring her here unless he had some idea she might be spending the night with Matt Hearne?

'He...he guessed.'

His brows rose in a derisive, incredulous arch. 'Guessed you were staying here? Is he a mind-reader? That's clever of him; how does he do that? You're only here because my mother was taken ill suddenly. It was all very spur of the moment—how could Heston possibly have guessed?'

She fought to sound normal, relaxed, but knew she wasn't managing it. Her voice was husky, the words jerking out of her in spasms that betrayed her nervous tension. 'He's been trying to ring me at home and when he couldn't get an answer he decided to ring you to see if you knew where I was.'

'Why would he ring here? How would he know this number? Why not try my London flat?'

'He tried that first, got no reply, so he tried this number.'

'It sounds as if he was pretty sure you would be with me,' he drawled and although the tone was soft it was like being flicked with a whip.

What could she say to that? Her eyes lowered, her lashes a cloak to hide the distress in them.

'Jealous, was he?' The question was bitten out so sharply that she couldn't help jumping as if he had hit her.

'No!' she threw back, her chin tilting in angry denial, her green eyes seething. 'No, of course not! Will you stop suggesting there's something going on between me and Don?' She broke off, so furious words jammed up inside her, then snapped, 'Look, I work for Don. That's all. There's nothing else going on between us!'

He mocked in cool, deliberate disbelief, 'No? Then why does everyone think there is?'

'Who's everyone? Sara Heston?' she furiously slung at him and saw his face change, wariness enter his eyes. She had surprised him, he hadn't expected that question, he didn't have a clue that she knew about him and Sara.

Before he could recover, she contemptuously said, 'If we're talking about secret relationships, what about you and Sara? Are you her lover?'

He stared as if she were speaking a foreign language,

one he did not understand. 'What?' Then he suddenly moved, taking three long strides across the room to grab her by the shoulders.

Startled, she looked up at him, eyes wide and uneasy. The contact was electric, unsettling. He was much too close; a hot pulse began beating in her neck; she became intensely aware of him, of her own body.

'I saw her, saw both of you,' she breathlessly accused. 'Last night. Did you think I wouldn't hear her arrive? How long did she stay? All night? I know she was here a long time; I couldn't sleep, and I saw her car outside for hours, but it was gone when I woke up this morning.'

His mouth twisted angrily. 'Don't judge everybody else by your standards! We don't all sleep around.'

She flinched at the contempt in his voice, the coldness of his gaze.

'I just told you, I'm not...don't...' she stammered.

'I know, you're just one of his executives!'

'It's true!'

'But he thinks he owns you. Why should he think you were likely to be with me all night? Did he tell you to get me to sign this contract by seducing me?'

She bit down on her inner lip, stricken by the shrewdness of the guess.

'You should see your face,' Matt curtly told her. 'A real give-away, that expression.'

'I didn't try to do anything of the kind!' she furiously pointed out. 'Did I come on to you? Offer to...to...?'

'Sleep with me? No, but then, as you found out, I had a surprise visitor, didn't I? Sara. How do I know what might have happened if she hadn't turned up? God knows why Heston strays all the time when he has a wife like her. She came because she had heard my mother was ill. And no, she didn't hear that from me! Sara spends a lot of time raising money for charities. She's a wonderful woman, and knows a lot of people in the Essex health service, including Ann Brown, the surgeon who operated on my mother last night. She rang Sara to ask for help in raising money for a new operating theatre for the local hospital. While they were talking, Ann told Sara about my mother, because Ann knows Sara was a friend of my wife. She told Sara my mother was very ill, and fretting about Lisa, worrying that I'd have to get some strange nanny to take care of her. Ann was afraid all that worry would make my mother's blood pressure shoot up, and put her at risk. So Sara actually drove over here to offer to look after Lisa, to put my mother's mind at rest.'

Bianca had never felt so small in her life. She believed him, without question. There was the ring of truth in his voice, in his face. She had been way off course with her accusation; now she felt guilty.

'I'm sorry,' she whispered. 'I feel stupid, accusing you and Sara like that. It was just the surprise of seeing her arrive at that time of night. Then, when you brought my hot chocolate, you didn't say a word about her; I thought you didn't want me to know she was here.'

'I didn't,' he shrugged. 'She was taken aback when I told her you were here, and asked me not to tell you she was in the house. She thought you would tell her husband, and that would lead to trouble.'

Sara Heston had been quite right, Bianca grimly recognised. Don would have suspected her motives for driving all that way, at night, to offer Matt Hearne help with his child. It wasn't in Don's nature to think the best of anyone, even his own wife.

Eyeing her mockingly, Matt murmured, 'I notice you

don't argue. You know your boss very well, don't you? He has the lowest possible opinion of human nature. He would have been suspicious of Sara's motives. He doesn't deserve that wife of his.'

Jealousy bit into Bianca; she couldn't stop herself asking him hoarsely, 'Are you in love with her?'

His fingertips clenched on her shoulders, he looked down into her eyes angrily, his voice harsh as he muttered, 'Can't you even imagine a man admiring a woman, respecting her, being her friend, without sex entering into it? You keep denying that you're Heston's mistress—do you expect me to believe you when you obviously can't accept that Sara and I are just good friends?'

'You believe Don's my lover because that was what his wife told you!'

'No. I've seen you together, remember. I've seen the way he looks at you. Whether you've actually been to bed with him, I know the man wants you. It's written in his face, as clear as day.'

She couldn't deny it. Flushing, she whispered, 'I've never encouraged him!'

'You could hand in your notice.'

The withering note in his voice got under her skin. 'And abandon my career?' she bitterly said. 'I'm not likely to get such a good job again—women executives rarely climb as high as I have, get so much responsibility, such a chance to prove themselves. I enjoy my work. I'm grateful to Don for giving me the opportunity to do my job. Believe me, there are plenty of male executives who would love to see me go, would jump at grabbing my job.'

'If you stay there Heston will get you, sooner or later. He's famous for his patience and tenacity. What was it he said, at the Savoy, a couple of days ago? He always gets what he wants, in the end.'

She shivered. Yes, she knew Don was always there, waiting for her to weaken, waiting for his chance to get into her bed.

'He won't get me!'

'Sure about that? Maybe you secretly want him, too. You may have moral objections to sleeping with a married man, but that wouldn't stop you wanting him as much as he wants you. There might even be a sort of tormented pleasure in denying yourself what you want—teasing yourself as well as him—knowing that sooner or later you'll surrender.'

'No! That's sick. And it's a lie. I don't want him.'

His hands tightened their hold on her; he stared at her trembling lips intently. 'You're very passionate about it. Are you sure? With all that fire under your ice you can't be as cool towards Heston as you want me to believe.'

'Let go of me, will you?' She took a step backwards but Matt abruptly jerked her towards him again. Their bodies collided with an impact that made her breathing quicken, her heart race.

His hands slid down from her shoulders, gripped her back, propelling her even closer. In their brief struggle the towelling robe parted; she heard Matt's breath catch. He looked down at her supple, writhing body, the high, naked breasts with their hard pink nipples, the smooth pale skin of hip and thigh.

'You're so lovely,' he whispered, and then his head lowered and she felt his mouth silkily brushing her throat. 'No wonder Heston wants you. No man with blood in his veins could look at you and not want you. With bait like you it's very tempting to walk into his

trap.' His head came up and he looked at her with fire
in his eyes, then his mouth closed over hers.

Bianca tried to resist him, pulling her head back,
arching her body in his hands, her lips trying to stay
shut against the intimate invasion of his mouth, but the
kiss made her pulses go crazy, sent shock waves of
intense pleasure through her.

Her eyes closed, she swayed as if fainting, leaning
on him, her arms going round his neck. Matt's hands
explored under the open robe, caressing the smooth,
cool breasts, fingering the firm nipples, making her
groan and shudder. Deep inside her a burning, feverish
need began to build; she kissed him back hungrily,
stroking his nape under the soft brown hair, finding the
beating vein in the side of his neck, the hollow of his
throat, the pulse of her own blood beating in rhythm
with his.

She was so out of control that when there was an ear-
splitting yell from Lisa in some other room it was shat-
tering. They both jumped violently. Split apart, faces
hot, eyes glazed, bodies shuddering.

She saw Matt swallow convulsively, his mouth open,
his skin very flushed.

'Lisa,' he hoarsely said, as if she might not guess.

She couldn't speak at all, just nodded, her hands
shaking as she tied the belt of her robe, pulling the
lapels together to hide her nakedness again. She
couldn't meet his eyes. Tears began to burn beneath her
lowered lids. Coming back to ordinary life after the
wildness of that emotion was torture was unbearable.

'I'd better go and find out what's wrong.' Matt
moved jerkily towards the door.

As he vanished Bianca put her hands over her face.
Tears trickled down through her trembling fingers. Her

skin was wet within two seconds, her mouth dry as ashes.

He could have had her a moment ago. She wouldn't have resisted. One kiss and she was all his for the taking, yet they had only met for the first time two days ago!

He must despise her. She despised herself. All her life she had been cautious, cool, in control. Just now she had lost all that, had been his for the taking any time he wanted her.

What on earth must he be thinking?

Oh, but she knew that, didn't she? He believed Don had told her to seduce him. Matt had probably been testing that theory—making a pass at her to see if she resisted or not.

And she hadn't, had she? Far from resisting, she had given in to him so completely that now he would be certain she was the bait for Don's trap, and he was going to feel nothing but contempt for her.

CHAPTER SIX

WHEN he came back he held Lisa by the hand. Bianca found it impossible to meet his eyes. Her heart was still crashing violently against her ribs; she could scarcely breathe. Being in the same room as him after what had just happened between them was keeping her nerves stretched to the limit.

'Is she okay?' she huskily asked. 'Did she see a scary cartoon?'

'No, apparently a bird crashed into the window and fell down. She thought it was dead, but it came to while she was showing me and fluttered away.'

He sat Lisa at the kitchen table and gave her back her crayons and colouring book. 'Colour Daddy this parrot? That needs lots of colours.'

'Parrot. Bird. Bird not dead,' Lisa murmured, emptying her box of crayons on to the table.

'No, not dead,' Matt reassured.

'Me hungry. Lunch soon?'

Matt looked at his watch, his brows rising. 'Hungry already? What do you want for lunch?'

'Pizza, please.'

Out of the corner of her eye Bianca watched him turn, walk across the room with his graceful, loping stride to open the freezer into which he stared.

'Well, there's certainly some frozen pizza, so you can have that, with some salad.'

Lisa beamed.

'Keeping this child fed is a full-time occupation,' he

muttered in Bianca's direction. 'I don't know how my mother finds the energy—I've only been looking after her for a few hours and already I'm exhausted.'

He sounded so normal—how did he do that? One minute they had been in each other's arms, caught up in wild sensuality—now, only a short time later, he was doing a terrific impersonation of a man who had nothing on his mind but domestic duties! Hadn't that kiss meant anything to him? Some men seemed able to separate sex and emotion, but she never had. Sex wasn't some appetite she fed now and then. It meant far more than that to her.

Obviously it didn't to him—had all his capacity for loving died with his wife?

Her mind surged with pain, anger, bewilderment. If their lovemaking really had meant nothing but the chance of easy sex to him it was demoralising. She had met plenty of men like that, always ready to seize the opportunity of a quick sexual encounter—was Matt that sort of man? She would never have guessed it. He didn't give that impression. She didn't want to believe it.

But what else was she to think?

Those few minutes in his arms had changed her whole life, forced her to admit the sudden, tangled emotions she had begun to feel for him soon after meeting him. She had never believed in love at first sight, but there was no other way of describing what had hit her.

From the minute she had seen him across that restaurant just two days ago she had been living in a vortex, endlessly whirling in circles, engulfed and unable to escape. She couldn't even bring her brain to bear on what was happening, she no longer trusted her intelligence; it seemed incapable of dealing with the power of her emotions.

'More coffee?' he asked behind her and she started violently.

'What?'

'I'm going to have another cup of coffee—do you want one?'

'Oh…oh, yes, please.' She must pull herself together, stop behaving like an idiot. He must think she was a complete fathead—well, what else was he to think?

'What do you want for lunch?'

'Pizza will be fine for me, too.'

'And salad?'

She nodded, her mind still surging with distress. She wasn't acting rationally, she hadn't been talking sense since he met her. He must wonder why on earth Don Heston had put her into such a demanding, responsible job.

But he thought he knew, didn't he? He believed she was Don's mistress, which was why she had such a good job. He thought Don had been paying her for services rendered.

'Why are you staring at that wall in that strange fashion?' he drawled and she stiffened, looking round aggressively.

'Will you stop picking on me?'

His brows shot up. 'What?'

'You're always making fun of me!'

'All I did was ask why you were standing with your back to me, doing nothing but stare at the wall! Why are you snarling like an unfed tiger?'

'Tigress,' she corrected. 'I'm female.'

'Oh, I've noticed that,' he murmured, mockery glinting in his blue eyes.

Her face began to burn. 'And you can stop that, too!

I don't want you flirting with me, I've told you that before.'

'You're a difficult woman to get on with, aren't you? You snap at me, whatever I say. I've never had so many arguments in such a short time with anyone!'

She saw Lisa watching them, her small face blank, which, with children, usually meant they were very aware of what was going on around them but pretending that they were not. Reverting to French, Bianca said warningly, *'Pas devant l'enfant.'*

Matt's lashes flicked towards his little girl. He looked back at Bianca, nodding.

'Point taken.' He walked away to get the coffee and Bianca went to the table to sit down and look at the parrot Lisa was colouring. She really did have a good sense of colour. The bird was red, green, yellow, blue and orange; staggeringly vivid.

'That's lovely,' congratulated Bianca.

Her tongue sticking out between her lips in her concentration, Lisa looked down at her work with smug satisfaction, nodding.

Matt handed Bianca a mug of coffee; she sat down to drink it, right next to Lisa, using the child as a shield against her father.

The strategy did not work. Matt leaned on the back of Bianca's chair to look at his daughter's artwork.

'Beautiful.'

Lisa beamed at him.

She could not see his fingers busily stroking Bianca's hair and neck. Bianca turned her head to glare at him and he gave her a teasing smile.

Silently she mouthed, 'Don't do that!'

Silently he mouthed back, 'What?'

'You know what I mean!' she soundlessly said.

He opened his blue eyes wide. 'Oh, you mean this!' He stroked her hair again, then she felt his cool fingertips trailing seductively across her nape and a shiver ran down her spine.

The effect he had on her was more and more worrying.

He bent down. 'Don't you like it when I do that?' he whispered in her ear.

Lisa was staring at them, frowning. 'Are you playing a game? Why are you talking so I can't hear you, Daddy? I want to play.'

Matt laughed. 'Can you play I Spy? Okay, what am I looking at? It begins with a P...' He stared fixedly at her colouring book and she looked at it, too, gave a sudden squawk of triumph.

'I know...parrot; P for Parrot.'

'Clever girl,' Matt praised.

'Now me, Daddy. My turn.' Lisa looked around the room, chewing her lower lip in thought, then said, 'D for...'

'No, don't tell me, I have to guess. D for Daddy?'

She laughed, showing all her teeth. 'No!'

Bianca drank her coffee, only half her attention on their game, nervously smoothing her robe down over her knee when it slid up and she sensed Matt staring down at her bare thighs.

'I give up, you win,' Matt absently told his daughter. 'What was it?'

'D for Dog,' shouted Lisa excitedly.

Matt stared round the room. 'I can't see any dog.'

'It's in my colouring book, silly, Daddy.' Lisa turned the page to show him.

'You can't have something I can't see!'

'I seed it, Daddy. D for dog!'

'But I couldn't see it in your book, Lisa. You have to pick something I can see.'

'Don't want to play any more. I'm busy.' Lisa began to colour again with a sulky expression.

'Five minutes of conversation with her and I begin to feel I'm Alice in Wonderland,' Matt groaned.

Lisa's head came up again, she turned to look at her father. 'You can't be Alice, Daddy, you're a boy,' she reproved.

'You are so literal-minded!' Matt walked to the door, yawning and stretching, his long, supple body, eye-riveting. Very male. Bianca watched him through lowered lashes, her mouth dry. He did something drastic to her heartbeat. She must get away from him as soon as possible.

'I have some work to do—could you keep an eye on her for an hour or so?' he asked.

Bianca nodded.

'You don't mind?'

'Not at all,' she assured him. 'I like looking after her.'

He gave her one of his sudden, charming smiles, the skin around his very blue eyes wrinkling, his face full of warmth.

'Thanks, I'm very grateful. I promise I won't take more than an hour. If you need me Lisa will show you my study. When I've finished, I'll make the lunch.'

'Why don't you let me do that? Pizza and salad is okay for you, too, is it?'

'You're such a highly qualified executive I hesitate to ask you to do something as humdrum as cooking frozen pizza!' he teased. 'But if you're sure you don't mind?'

'Why should I mind if you don't? It's just something

that has to be done. We have to eat, somebody has to do it.'

'Well, thank you, then.'

A few minutes after he had left the washing machine completed its cycle, so she moved all her clothes into the tumble-dryer, and began making a salad. There was a little lettuce, a few tomatoes, but she found a jar of pickled beetroot in the cupboard and a tin of peeled, sliced mandarin oranges, so she managed to make a rather strange but interesting salad mixture.

Before she cooked the pizza she sat with Lisa at the table and told her a story about elephants lost in the jungle who found their way home by following a brightly coloured parrot. Lisa pretended to be the elephant, making trumpeting noises, blowing down her nose.

Bianca put the oven on and while it was heating up she and Lisa played a game of noughts and crosses. Bianca had to work hard to make sure Lisa won as the child had little idea how the game should be played.

A quarter of an hour later Bianca put the pizza in the oven, and laid the table with Lisa's help. When the pizza was cooked Bianca sent Lisa to ask her father to come along for lunch.

The kitchen was full of a delicious smell of hot cheese and tomato by the time Matt and Lisa came back. Bianca got the pizza out of the oven and cut the big circle into three wedges, then served it on the plates. She gave the smallest piece to Lisa and placed it in front of her before adding some of the mixed salad. She had found some natural *fromage frais* in the fridge which would serve as a dressing.

'Help yourself to salad,' she told Matt as he washed his hands before sitting down.

'Smells great. I don't often eat pizza—do you?'

'Not often,' she confessed. This one was delicious—a crispy base, rich tomato sauce topped with thick, melting cheese—and the salad made a perfect contrast.

'Cool,' Lisa said, through a mouthful of food.

Matt averted his eyes. 'Don't talk with your mouth full!'

Bianca poured a mug of cold milk for the little girl who took it in both hands and drank noisily. From Matt's expression he didn't enjoy that, either. It was all too obvious that he didn't spend much time with his child. He had a lot to learn about small children.

Lisa began to yawn as they finished lunch. 'Time for her nap,' Matt said with what was obvious relief.

'No. Not tired,' Lisa complained, but he picked her up and carried her upstairs while Bianca cleared the table and loaded the dishwasher.

When he came back, he told her flatly that when his daughter woke up he would be taking Lisa to stay with Sara Heston for a few days.

'She very kindly offered to take care of her, and she's used to children; Lisa will be fine with her.'

Bianca felt a rush of resentment—how could he pass Lisa over to a woman she didn't even know? Or did she? Had Sara Heston been here, met Lisa before? What exactly was the relationship between her and Matt?

'Lisa would rather be with you, especially at the moment! She needs reassurance, not to be dumped on someone else.'

He flushed angrily. 'I know that, but, thanks to your firm, I'm up to my ears in work. I can't spare the time to take care of her.'

The tumble-dryer came to a sudden stop. Tense and irritated, Bianca turned to take the clothes out.

'I'll get dressed now,' she said stiffly. 'If you're taking Lisa to the Hestons' place maybe you could drop me at a railway station *en route*?'

'I brought you, I'll take you back,' he snapped. 'I shall be going up to London myself, anyway.'

She didn't trust herself to reply. Turning on her heel, she walked out, carrying her clothes with her. She took her time getting dressed, found her handbag, her red cashmere wrap, then sat on the bed and stared out of the window for a while, brooding over Matt's behaviour and feeling intense sympathy for his child. She knew how it felt to have your father ignore you, dump you, walk away from you. How could Matt be so thoughtless and insensitive?

When she went back downstairs there was no sign of Matt—presumably he was working again.

An hour later Lisa began to call out and Bianca ran upstairs to get her up. Matt appeared a moment later. The little girl was very flushed and bright-eyed. She held her arms up to her father who lifted her out of her cot.

'I've packed a bag of clothes for her. We'll leave at once.'

The child's bedroom looked as if a bomb had hit it; drawers were open, clothes inside them ruffled and tumbled. Matt must have turned the room upside down in his packing.

'Want kanga,' Lisa demanded, so they had to find the kangaroo before they left, but eventually they got her into the car and drove away. Lisa sat in her car seat, in the back, staring out of the window, babbling to herself.

'I spy...T for tree...H for horse...' She did not invite either of them to play the game with her. She was clearly far too used to her own company, and could amuse herself alone for hours.

'Do you know the way to the Hestons' house?' Bianca asked Matt, who shot her a look through his thick, silky brown lashes, which glinted bright gold in the afternoon sunlight. He had changed into a cream shirt, dark brown linen jacket and matching trousers, very casual with the expensive look of good designer wear.

They hadn't been bought off the hanger in a chain store, that was certain. Fitting him perfectly, they streamlined his lean body, gave him charismatic good looks.

Bianca averted her eyes again. Looking at him was dangerous. She must try never to do it again.

'They live in Buckinghamshire, but it won't take more than a couple of hours to get there.'

'But then you have to drive me all the way back to town. Aren't you going to visit your mother?'

He shook his head. 'I rang the hospital half an hour ago. She's still suffering from the after-effects of the anaesthetic, and very drowsy, so they asked me not to come today.'

Distracted, Bianca frowned in concern. 'I'm sorry, I hope she's okay by tomorrow.'

'The ward sister assured me it was not unusual with older patients for the anaesthetic to cause a few problems. She said my mother was going to be fine; it just takes a little longer to get over an operation at her age.'

'K for kangaroo,' said Lisa in the back. She held the toy up in the air. 'See, Daddy?'

'Yes, I see, darling. K for kangaroo.'

They drove on with the child chattering to herself in the back.

'Have you been to the Hestons'?' he asked. Bianca shook her head.

He looked as if he didn't believe her. 'Not even while Sara and the children were in the West Indies on holiday last year?'

'No.'

'When she got back Sara found a couple of things around the house that made her think he had had some woman down there.'

'And she thought it was me?'

'You were chief suspect,' he agreed with a twist of the mouth.

'Well, it wasn't me and I have no idea who it could have been.'

She was bristling at his sardonic, derisive tone. Who did he think he was, accusing her like this? He claimed he wasn't in love with Sara Heston, but he was obviously close to her, believed whatever she said.

He disliked Don in a very personal way—not simply because their firm was trying to acquire his company. She suspected he had always disliked Don; it was one of those instinctive animosities. Don probably felt the same—did he suspect his wife of being unfaithful with Matt Hearne? No, she doubted it. Don's ego wouldn't allow for the possibility of his wife preferring any other man.

But how could she be sure? She couldn't work either of them out—Don or Matt. Matt Hearne certainly still believed that she was Don's mistress, and made no secret of his contempt for her, for both of them.

As for Don, he had been chasing her ever since she joined the firm—an insistent, determined pursuit, refusing to accept her rejections.

Yet he had suggested she seduce Matt Hearne, to

persuade him to sign their deal! If he had ever cared anything for her, how could he? She felt sickness coil inside her stomach. There was only one explanation. Don saw her as one of his disposable assets. He didn't think of her as a person with rights and feelings and a mind of her own. He saw her as a sexual object he could use for his own ends. An object he desired and wanted to own in every sense of the word.

Her skin turned icy as she considered the mere possibility of letting him into her bed.

She would rather die. The thought of his hands on her made her shudder. She knew that if he even touched her she would throw up.

Startled, she realised that her attitude to him had changed radically over the past forty-eight hours.

Her rejection of his passes until now had been based on sheer instinct. She hadn't thought it through, simply held him at bay, saying no, without losing her temper or getting upset. If anyone had asked her before this weekend she would have said she liked and admired Don. But for her a married man was out of bounds. Even if she had been seriously attracted, she wouldn't have had an affair with him, with any man who wasn't free. But she had still liked Don as a person. In fact, she would have said, as she had to Matt only a few hours ago, that Don treated her with respect and was a great boss to work for, not to mention a nice guy.

Why did she feel so differently about him now?

Had the change begun when he'd asked her to seduce Matt and implied that her brief relationship with Harry Mistell had been phoney, meant only to make their deal with Harry's father easier? That had been so insulting. She had been outraged—who wouldn't have been? The idea of being used as sexual bait would be humiliating and degrading to any woman.

But had he meant it?

When he rang her a short time ago he had seemed taken aback when she answered the phone. As if he couldn't believe she had really gone to Essex with Matt. Maybe it had all been Don's idea of a joke? Was that why he had seemed so amazed to discover that she had apparently spent the night with Matt?

He had been so taken aback that he hadn't even been able to talk to her, had rung off without saying anything. He must have rung from the plane on his mobile, unless his plane had been delayed and he was stuck at Heathrow. Well, if he rang again he would not find her at Matt's; he would have to start looking elsewhere again.

Matt whispered, 'She's fast asleep,' and Bianca glanced at Lisa, smiling at the sight of her, limp and pink-faced, sound asleep; her thumb was in her mouth, her eyes shut.

'She looks so sweet.'

'Looks aren't everything,' Matt said, shooting Bianca a sideways glance she did not feel was complimentary. She refused to ask him what that was supposed to mean. It would only encourage him.

They drove through heavy traffic on the M25, London's orbital motorway, always crowded, day and night, running as it did through all the suburbs around the capital.

At last they turned north on to the M1, the great artery heading out of London, but half an hour later they left that motorway, too, heading for the Buckingham-shire village where Don's family lived.

She stared out of the window, watching the shimmer

of sunlight low on the horizon. English trees stood on the edges of fields—oak and ash, just coming into leaf—and in gardens they passed the burnished bronze of maple and the pink of apple blossom not yet blown off the branch. The air had that sweet, heavy, drowsy scent of approaching night.

'I'm curious,' Matt suddenly said, making her jump. 'How does it feel to work for a shark-like company that exists by constantly eating up smaller firms, throwing people out of their jobs, stripping assets, just to make a profit?'

'That isn't fair! TTO is a go-ahead, successful electronics company itself—it knows the market, is on the ball where new inventions are concerned. When it buys a company like yours it's always because it can see how that company would fit in with it, how they're going to click together, because they have synergy.'

'Synergy?' he sarcastically repeated. 'Oh, yes, of course. Heston would use words like that.'

'All it means is that our companies would fit together!'

'I know what it means, and I can see what Heston thinks we could do for his firm, but what good would it do us?'

'TTO makes a lot of money for its shareholders, which would be good for your shareholders if they agreed to a deal—and with TTO backing your product would have a much bigger share of the market than it does at the moment.'

'But I'd have lost my company, so what good would that do me?'

'I've explained. TTO want you to come on board, we want you working for us, you wouldn't lose anything.'

'Except my independence, except my freedom, except my ability to make decisions I believe in!'

'You would still be free to make decisions! You would be in charge of how your invention developed!'

He laughed. 'Do you think I'm stupid? Of course I wouldn't. Heston would make the decisions. I would be expected to jump when he told me to, work at what he said I must—I'd have no freedom or responsibility at all. Be honest, for once, Bianca—what freedom or choice do you have?'

She couldn't deny anything he had said. Soberly, she admitted, 'Very little, but then I'm not a policy-maker; my job is to negotiate, persuade, convince. I have never operated on any higher level. Only Don is in charge of the company's overall decisions. After all, he is the boss.'

'And he owns you.'

She stiffened. 'I told you, no! He doesn't.'

'What exactly did he say to you on the phone?'

'Nothing.'

'He must have said something. What was it?''

She hesitated. 'Just that he had been trying to get hold of me in London and...'

He waited as she fell silent, then said drily, 'And what were you doing at my home in the country, and had you been with me all night?'

She stared out of the window, not answering.

'Did he suggest you slept with me to get me to agree to this deal?'

She didn't answer that, either. She was not lying, but she couldn't admit the truth, either.

'I thought so,' Matt said. 'Now, tell me about Harry Mistell.'

She tensed, her hands gripped together in her lap. 'No.'

'I've heard all the gossip. How you and he started dating, and then his father signed that deal with Heston, and suddenly you and young Mistell were no longer an item. Everyone believes you played him on your line until their family firm was landed, then you chucked the guy back into the river and walked off. Not very pretty.'

'Not true, either!' she angrily denied. 'It was Harry who broke off our friendship…'

'Friendship?' he repeated in sardonic tones. 'Is that what it was? Just good friends, eh? Not lovers?'

'Friends,' she said through tight lips. 'Just friends.'

'So why did Mistell drop you?'

'He heard gossip—it wasn't true, but he refused to believe me.'

'Gossip about you and Heston?'

She nodded. 'But it was all lies. I told him it wasn't true, but he wouldn't listen.'

'Stupid guy. You're better off without someone like that. If he doesn't trust you, or listen to what you tell him, you would never have been happy with him.'

'I suppose so. But I was very upset—it isn't pleasant being called a liar, and a cheat, or accused of being somebody's mistress.'

'Who told young Mistell about you and Heston?'

'He wouldn't say.'

'Heston himself, probably.'

Bianca's jaw dropped; she turned in her seat to stare at him. 'Don?'

'Well, he'd got this deal signed, so young Mistell no longer mattered, and Heston wanted to use you as bait again.' Matt slid her a mocking sideways glance. 'With me, for instance. He probably already had it in mind to acquire my company, and get you to persuade me to sign. But first he had to get rid of young Mistell.'

Hurriedly, she protested, 'I haven't been trying to…to…'

'Seduce me?' His blue eyes glinted. 'I'd be prepared to bet he asked you to, though?'

Bianca was silent. He watched her in his driving mirror, saw the confusion and uncertainty, the shifting emotions in her face.

'He did, didn't he? He made it pretty obvious, at the Savoy the other day—he's good with hidden meanings. Telling me you were available—what else did it mean? He meant me to understand that you were mine for the taking, if I wanted you. How often has he put you up for bidders, like that?'

Tears pricked her eyes. 'Never. I was so shocked and embarrassed, listening to him, being so obvious… I told him I wasn't on offer to anybody, I'd rather resign.'

'Let me guess what he said…that you didn't actually have to go to bed with me, just let me think you might!'

Her face was hot, her mouth dry. He might have been present, heard Don talking! Self-respect wouldn't let her lie to him.

Her silence dragged on. Matt took one hand from the wheel and softly touched her hands, clenched together in her lap.

'You can't go on working for the man, you know that, don't you? You said he treats you with respect. Well, maybe he did, once, but not any more. Now he's treating you like a hooker and sooner or later he's going to try to force you into bed with him. You've got to give him notice and get away from him, even if it means you won't earn so much.'

'Yes, I know, I've been working my way round to

facing up to that,' she bleakly admitted. 'I love my job, but I don't like the way Don has been acting lately. It all really started when I began going out with Harry. Don turned weird.'

'You really liked young Mistell?'

'Yes, I told you, I didn't date him because of the merger, I dated him because I liked him a lot.'

'Heston realised it might get serious—and turned jealous?'

She sighed, shrugging. 'I don't know. But he's been different, ever since. I used to like him so much, too; it's all very sad.'

Matt was silent, staring straight ahead, his profile razor-sharp and unusually serious, the bones of cheek and jaw set rigidly.

'We're nearly there. When we arrive, I think you had better stay in the car while I take Lisa into the house. We don't want an unpleasant scene, do we?'

She shivered. 'Sara hates me that much?'

'Let's just say you aren't her favourite person.'

'But the gossip is all lies! If I explained…'

'She wouldn't believe you. She's quite sure her husband is having an affair with you. Don't forget she sees another side of Don. If she thinks he's in love with you, maybe she's right?'

'I just told you he isn't!'

'I know, and I believe you, but I'm not a jealous wife whose husband no longer seems to care about her. Just stay in the car, Bianca, please? I don't want Lisa having to witness nasty scenes. Come to that, I wouldn't enjoy them myself.'

They drove up a long, curving gravel drive under lime trees. Ahead of them a white house shimmered; it was larger than Bianca had expected, older, too, built in a Colonial style, the walls stucco, set graciously with drooping willow trees on either side, with a balcony along the front, a portico in the centre, and steps up to the black oak front door.

'What an amazing place!' Bianca breathed.

Matt pulled up and gazed at the house. 'You've never been here?'

'I told you. No. Never.' Why did he always doubt what she said to him? He must have a very low opinion of her honesty.

Matt got out of the car and went round to undo Lisa's car seat belt. She woke up, making a whiny noise.

'Shh, baby. Go back to sleep.' He collected a small suitcase from the back seat—he must have packed it while she and Lisa were out for their walk! Why hadn't he told her hours ago that he meant to bring his little girl to Sara? Why leave it till the last moment?

He lifted Lisa into his arms, and carried her up the steps to the front door.

It opened before he knocked. Bianca caught sight of Sara Heston briefly, elegant in a cream linen dress, her hair brushed around her face. She was too busy looking at Matt and his child to notice Bianca in the car parked outside. Matt carried Lisa inside, and the front door shut.

Bianca stared around the beautiful garden; it was carefully kept, with smooth lawns, well trimmed shrubs, borders rich with budding peonies, white and red roses, blue bearded iris, and nearby the sweet scent of lilac and stocks drifting to her nostrils. She suddenly saw a curtain swing back in an upstairs window, then Don's face showed, staring down at her, his features set in rage. She stared up in disbelief, doubting her own eyes.

The curtain closed again, he vanished, but a moment

later the front door opened and he rushed out, leapt down the steps and pulled open the car door to glare in at her.

'Don? What are you doing here? Why aren't you on your way to Australia?'

'I didn't go, obviously. Why are you here with Hearne?'

'He's taking me back to London. But first we brought his little girl here—your wife offered to look after her because his mother is in hospital. We were on our way to a restaurant for dinner when he got a call on his car phone to say his mother had been taken ill and his little girl had nobody to take care of her, so I offered to help him with her until he could get someone else.'

'He doesn't miss a trick, does he? Gave you this sob story, then talked you into bed to comfort him, I suppose?'

Her face burned. 'I didn't sleep with him! Look, why aren't you going to Australia?

He laughed unpleasantly, his face pale except for two patches of angry red in the middle of his cheeks. 'I was just off to the airport when I was served with divorce papers! So I cancelled my trip and came down here to find out what the hell Sara thought she was doing! And do you know what she told me?' He bent to stare into her eyes, his face working violently. 'She said she wanted a divorce because I was unfaithful to her! I said it wasn't true, there was nobody else in my life.' He met Bianca's cool stare and snarled, 'Well, there isn't, at the moment! I haven't had an affair for quite some time, and I told her so. Then she said she was going to name you!'

'Me?' Aghast, Bianca broke out, 'But didn't you tell her...?'

'Of course I did! I told her we had never slept to-gether, so she wouldn't be able to get any evidence, it was all in her imagination, and I could prove it. I said I would fight a divorce, I wouldn't agree to one—which would mean she would have to wait for it to be granted. She got so upset that I realised she had lied to me; she had a very different reason for wanting to be free.'

Bianca's mind leapt with jealous suspicion. 'What reason?' she hoarsely asked.

'Isn't it obvious? She's in love with someone else. I tried to ring her last night, but got no reply. I kept trying until gone midnight, when I went to bed. So I asked where she had been at that time of night, and she told me she had been at Matt Hearne's place.'

Bianca bit her lip—should she tell him she had seen Sara there?

Before she could decide, Don had angrily added, 'Oh, she had some cock-and-bull story about offering to take care of his little girl, but nobody drives all that way at that hour, for a reason like that. Why wouldn't she just ring him? It hit me like an express train—she wants a divorce so that she can marry Matt Hearne!'

CHAPTER SEVEN

IT WAS as if an earthquake had suddenly hit; the sky swooped down over her, everything was spinning dizzily, the trees hazy black shapes, the house seeming to sway to and fro with terrifying instability. Her face pale and cold, she stared at Don.

'She...she's going to divorce you and marry...Matt?' Her voice broke, because she couldn't say the words; she didn't want to believe it, she was having trouble just breathing.

'Yes,' Don ground out between clenched teeth. 'That bastard has stolen my wife! I suppose he thought it would pay me back for trying to grab his company. Tit for tat.'

Bianca shook her head, which felt as if it was perched perilously on top of her neck and might fall off.

'Matt swore nothing was going on between them.'

Don's eyes narrowed, shiny with rage. 'Why?'

'Why?' she blankly repeated, confused, not understanding the question.

Impatiently, Don snapped, 'Why did he swear it? It can't just have come up in conversation, for heaven's sake! Did you ask him if they were lovers? What made you think they might be? You must have noticed something to put the idea into your head!'

It dawned on her that she could have been hoodwinked. Matt had been so convincing, oh, so very convincing! But had he been lying, all the time? He had

114

taken her in——but then hadn't she been eager to believe him?

'I saw her at his house and…' She stopped on a painful intake of air, not adding the rest. How could she tell him she had seen his wife in Matt's arms, seen Matt kiss Sara Heston, heard her tell him, 'I had to come…'? That would merely confirm Don's suspicions.

'And?' demanded Don. 'What was going on? Something must have made you suspect they were having an affair.'

Bianca couldn't help sympathising with Sara. Don had hardly been the perfect husband; he had neglected his wife and family for years, had affairs, chased Bianca herself ever since she joined his firm. Maybe he deserved to lose his wife. How many women would put up with neglect, indifference and infidelity for years?

I wouldn't, she thought. Don should have realised that sooner or later the worm would turn and his wife would decide she had had enough.

His angry face showed that Sara's announcement that she was going to divorce him had shaken him to his roots, but was he ready yet to face up to his own responsibility for her decision? Look at the way he had protested that he wasn't having an affair at the moment! He seemed to think that all that mattered was that he was innocent, this time, and his wife couldn't prove otherwise. But what about the relationships he had had in the past? Didn't he understand what the pain and humiliation must have done to Sara?

Don saw everything from his own point of view. He was a selfish, self-obsessed man. He didn't even consider looking at life through his wife's eyes. Maybe he would, eventually, as the divorce bit into him——but it would be too late.

While he was relentlessly working to get Matt Hearne's company it would never have occurred to him that, behind his back, Matt might have been stealing his wife, and finding it easy to do so because Don had long ago ceased to show her he loved her.

But his angry reaction to the threat of the divorce proved he had loved her once. Maybe, deep down, he still did so? She sensed that he was thinking on his feet and working out his best strategy for coping with losing Sara. He had always been able to handle opposition in business. He was a street fighter; he wouldn't just accept his wife's decision. He was too tough to give up easily. That was why he ran the company so well.

He had been a good boss to work for, but she didn't have much of an opinion of him as a human being. His private life was a shambles.

He had always ruled the roost at home—it wouldn't have occurred to him that Sara might one day stand up to him, defy him.

His face dark red, a tiny tic flickering under one eye, he said, 'She tells me she's going to go for half of everything I own!' His jaw worked, his breathing thick.

Sara's threat had really got under his skin.

'She might well get it, too,' Bianca thought aloud. 'Modern divorce law means that the wife gets the house and a fair share of the family assets.'

'Fair share?' Don snarled. 'Fair share? I built this company up, not her! How can it be fair for her to grab it away from me? All these years she just spent my money, lived it up down here, went to parties, bought designer clothes, sent her kids to public school.'

Suddenly they were Sara's kids, not his! noted Bianca. Softly, she said, 'Ah, but she made a home for you and your children, she gave parties for your clients, didn't she? She helped you all she could on the social side of the business, so I've heard, especially in the beginning. Divorce courts take account of all that.'

Don didn't like that. 'She's hardly even set foot inside the offices! How can it be fair for her to steal my company from me? If that's the law, it's insanity.' He stopped talking, stared at his house, breathing thickly. 'She'll get my home, and the kids, too, probably, and on top of that, I could end up working for her—for my own wife! Well, I won't do it. I am not working for a woman!'

'You won't get a choice, if that's what the court decides.' Bianca had begun to enjoy the situation. It was gratifying to see Don in such a fix.

'You sound as if you think it's funny!' he snapped. 'It isn't, Bianca. Not funny at all.'

'Well, look on the bright side, Don. As Sara knows nothing about how the company works she'll probably settle for her share as a lump sum.'

He didn't seem to find any comfort in that thought. 'My God! I'd have to borrow the money to buy her out, get myself into debt.'

'I'm sure the lawyers will work out a deal.'

'And take a huge bite out of my money at the same time! You know what greedy sharks lawyers are!' His eyes narrowed in furious thought. 'Sara would never have thought of this on her own. She's never had a head for business, never been interested in the company. I know who's behind this—that bastard Hearne!'

He was probably right, thought Bianca grimly. Matt was clever, shrewd, and, judging by the way he had behaved to her, an opportunist who saw every angle and took every advantage.

'Bastard!' Don seethed.

Silently Bianca agreed with him.

'He's getting his own back,' Don muttered. 'I tried to take over his company so this is his revenge. He's taking my wife, and he probably hopes to get my company, too. He's turned the tables on me.'

'A neat trick!'

Don glared at her. 'Do you realise that this could end up with Hearne in control of TTO?'

Don did not seem to find the irony in the situation in the least bit funny.

'Well, I'm not going to let him get away with it,' he snarled.

'How will you stop him?'

Don ran a hand over his sweating face, then looked sharply at Bianca. 'Did you know? Are you against me, Bianca? Have you been plotting with those two?'

'Of course I haven't! Don't get paranoid, Don. Everybody isn't conspiring against you.'

She was beginning to be concerned about the way he looked. She could see perspiration springing out on his face and neck, making his white shirt cling to his body. His light summer suit, meant for this Australian trip, was damp with sweat too, and there were enlarged blue veins in his neck. He looked like a man on the verge of something disastrous.

'Don, you look terrible; calm down! If you aren't careful you'll make yourself ill.'

He wasn't listening to her, though—only to the fury inside his own head.

'Somebody in the company had to be feeding Hearne information!'

'Oh, don't be ridiculous, Don! Why would I do that?'

'Don't try to kid me. I'm the expert on take-overs; I've had one of Hearne's directors on my payroll for a couple of months, giving me inside information. I always do get someone from the other firm on my side, if I can.'

She was astonished, and indignant that he had kept that news from her. 'You never told me that!'

'Of course I didn't. I know you. You'd have been shocked and said it wasn't ethical, or moral, or something! But buying someone from the other firm can save a lot of time and money, let you know exactly what the other side is thinking.'

His glare hated her. 'I never thought *you'd* betray me. You have, though, haven't you? Or you wouldn't be here with him!'

Without warning he leaned into the car and grabbed Bianca's arm, pulled her out of her seat.

'Stop it, Don. You're hurting me!' she hissed at him.

He didn't let her go, he intensified his grip, his fingers digging into her arm. 'You're coming with me!'

'Stop it, Don! Are you mad?'

'He's bought you, hasn't he? That's what's happened. What's he paying you?'

'Nothing. Don't be stupid.' She wrenched her arm free, rubbing the red mark he had made on her skin. 'Look what you've done! I know you're upset, but don't take it out on me!'

He looked at her with rage in his eyes, in his sweating, reddened face.

'I've been living in a fool's paradise, trusting my wife, trusting you. But not any more. From now on I'm playing hardball. I pay your salary, you come with me.'

From behind them they heard the front door open, then Matt shouted, 'Bianca! What's going on?'

She turned, her mouth opening to call for help, but Don muttered to her, 'He's my wife's lover, remember!'

She shut her mouth again. What if he was right? Don might be a ruthless bastard, and slightly crazy at the moment, but it was beginning to look as if Matt was a liar, too, and just as ruthless.

Hurriedly Don said, 'Whatever he's paying you, I'll double.'

'Oh, stop talking about money,' she snapped. 'Is that all you understand?'

Matt began running, his feet churning up gravel. Urgently, Don reminded her, 'From the day you joined our firm you've been on the fast track, because I've been promoting you all the way. Are you going to turn your back on me now, when I need all the help I can get?'

It was true; she owed her entire career to Don. If Sara Heston was planning to take the company away from her husband what choice did Bianca have? Her loyalties lay with Don in this fight. He had done so much for her, she owed him her support now.

Once this crisis was over, she was resigning, however. First, she would look for another job, of course. That would only be sensible. She didn't want to eat into her savings.

Don grabbed her hand. 'Run!'

She obeyed him, got into the passenger seat of his car while he ran round to get behind the wheel before Matt reached them.

'Bianca, where are you going?' Matt shouted through the window as Don started the engine.

She didn't answer, or even look at him, her face averted. Don put his foot down and the car shot forward, churning gravel noisily. Matt ran beside her, keeping level with the car, shouting, but she didn't even hear what he was saying; she was too distressed, tears stinging behind her lids, her mouth trembling, her shaking hands locked in her lap.

She was so sick of men lying to her, cheating her, trying to manipulate her. Matt was just another man she couldn't trust.

Don drove away at speed. In the wing mirror Bianca caught a glimpse of Matt standing there, staring after them, then the car turned a bend and all she could see were the lime trees at that end of the drive, lit by the car's brilliant headlights, glossy green heart-shaped leaves with paler undersides, drooping pale yellow flowers spinning in the wind, thick branches descending to the ground, making a secret bower within. In the gleam of the artificial light they looked ghostly and she shivered.

She opened the window to snatch air into her lungs and the scent of the limes made her head swim. Closing her eyes she let her head fall back against the seat. She had never felt so unhappy in her life and she knew it would be a long time before she got over this feeling of betrayal. Matt had lied to her. She would never be able to bear the smell of lime trees again.

'You're heading back to London?' she wearily asked Don.

'Uh huh,' he grunted. 'You and I have work to do tonight.'

Her eyes flew open, she threw him a startled look. 'What do you mean, work?'

Don still looked terrible. He had aged, overnight. He had always seemed younger than his actual years. Now he looked older.

'I shall have to talk to all our major shareholders. We can't let them hear about this from Sara's lawyers, or the press. We'll go direct to the office, you can get the list for me, and line up calls.' His face was locked in the bitter intensity of battle; bones tight, mouth clenched, eyes hard. She knew that expression.

Don was a fighter; he wouldn't give his wife an easy victory. Did Sara realise what she was taking on? Did Matt?

'Don, it's a Saturday night!' she pointed out. 'Most of them will be at dinner, or at a party, and even if they're at home they aren't going to be very happy about getting a business call. Leave it until Monday.'

'It can't wait. I have to stop Hearne and Sara at once before it's too late, and to do that I need allies.'

'Shouldn't you talk to your lawyers first?'

He turned his head to glare furiously at her. 'Will you stop trying to tell me what to do? This is my company, and my wife. I know what I'm doing.'

She fell silent and for an hour didn't say anything as they drove towards London. The motorway was half empty now; people were driving out of London, not into it. Don's car ate up the miles at speed.

Only as they actually began to enter the capital did Bianca venture to say quietly, 'Don, I'm very tired, and you look tired, too. Wouldn't it be wiser to wait until tomorrow morning? I'll work all day, if you need me, but not tonight.'

Don showed his teeth, growling like an angry dog. 'I have to save my company.'

'Not tonight, Don, there's nothing you can really do until tomorrow. Sleep on it and maybe you'll have worked something out.'

'In the morning it could be too late!'

'Of course it won't! A divorce takes a long time, even if both parties are agreed—and you don't want a divorce, do you?'

'You bet I don't! And I'll fight it up to the last post.'

'I'm sure you will,' she soothed, glad to see he was calming down a little. 'But even so, it isn't your shareholders you need to talk to, or even your lawyers—it's still your wife who is the key to this. Sara's obviously hurt and angry—you need to talk to her.'

He erupted, his face red with temper again. 'What good do you think that will do? I tell you Matt Hearne is behind all this. Talking won't solve anything. I've got to work out how to fight him.'

'Don, stop shouting and start thinking! You must work out your problems with Sara if you want to save your marriage. That means you have to stop getting angry and calm down, then talk to her—or rather, listen to her. I can't believe she really wants to break up your home, upset your children. Divorce is so final. Try to persuade her to give you another chance.'

'There's no time. I still have to make this Australian trip.'

She couldn't believe her ears. 'For once in your life, Don, put your wife first! Australia will still be there in a few days. Now is the time for you to concentrate on Sara.'

He looked uncertain, which was a first for Don—she had never seen him in a state like this. Maybe he cared more about Sara than he had ever admitted to himself? He had just wanted to have his cake and eat it, too?

'I suppose I could have a shot at talking her round,' he said doubtfully, frowning ahead into the bright lights of London's streets, thronged with people on a Saturday night.

'No, Don! Don't talk to her—listen! And you could start by telling her you love her. Tell her she shocked you into realising how you felt about her. You do care about her, don't you? Why else are you so horrified by the idea of losing her?'

His skin reddened. 'Of course I care about her,' he roughly said. 'We've been married for years, we're a family, we have wonderful children we both love.' He paused, his face confused, and raked a hand through his curly brown hair. 'I can't believe this is happening. I can't imagine being without her.'

'Then tell her so!'

'But even if she listens I shall still have to go to Australia soon, and while I'm away Hearne might get to her again.'

'You aren't thinking straight, Don. It's obvious—ask her to go to Australia with you. You never take her on trips, do you? Now is a good time to start. If she's with you, she can't be with Matt Hearne.'

His face changed. 'I hadn't thought of that, but you're right. It's a great idea. That's what I'll do—ask her to come to Australia! We can make it a holiday once I've finished my business meetings.'

'And make a fuss of her out there, spend time with her, have long, romantic dinners together, buy her roses, tell her you're sorry, tell her you love her, and you couldn't bear to lose her.'

They were in Pimlico by then. Pulling up outside the tall Victorian house, he turned to look at her. She had never imagined seeing Don look this way—uncertain, unsure of himself, almost a little lost.

'You really think that would work?'

'If you mean it, yes. Don, for heaven's sake—forget tactics. Forget winning—this isn't a war. This is personal.'

'It's both,' he said glumly. 'Personal, and a war.'

She gave him a long, serious stare, searching his face

for clues. 'I know you haven't been faithful to her, but you don't want to lose her, do you?'

'Of course I don't,' he grunted. 'And I don't want to lose my company, either!'

Sighing, Bianca said, 'I shouldn't mention that, Don. That's the last thing she'll want to hear. Talk about your feelings, not your business, for once. Forget the firm. You've concentrated on work for far too long. Sara is a woman; the only thing she wants to hear about is how you feel, that you really care about her. Tell her you need her, you're sorry you've taken her for granted for so long, you never will again.'

Flushed, he growled, 'Oh, for heaven's sake, Bianca, you'll tell me to play a guitar under her window next! Look, okay, I do love her, in my own way—we've been together for a long time and I'd miss her if she went, but I'm not the sentimental type, you know. She knows that, too; she won't believe me if I lay it on with a trowel.'

Bianca couldn't help smiling at his embarrassment. 'She will if you tell her how jealous you are of Matt Hearne!'

'I didn't say I was jealous of that bastard!'

'But you are, aren't you?'

He looked away, his body language petulant, and didn't answer.

'Tell Sara she has shaken you to your roots by saying she doesn't love you any more; you thought you could always rely on her love.'

His face was sullen. 'Oh, sure! And then she'll have a good laugh.'

'Not if you mean it when you say it. Not if you show her you really love her. Stop hiding your feelings. Let them show. The point is—do you care, Don? If you don't, let her go. Don't be a dog in the manger. Even if that means you lose a lot of money. But if you do still love her, now is the time to tell her so.'

There was no point in saying any more; let him think about it. 'Goodnight, Don,' she said, opening the car door.

He grabbed her arm. 'You really think that's what I should do? You think it would work?'

She nodded. 'So long as Sara really loves you, deep down, and I think she does. She has stayed with you all this time; she must feel something for you. If I were you, I'd even go tonight, right away, while you're in the mood.'

'What if Hearne's with her?' he muttered. 'I'll kill him if he is!'

'That wouldn't be a good idea,' she said, laughing a little angrily, because she was so angry with Matt. She felt like killing him herself. Drily she added, 'But it wouldn't hurt to punch him on the nose. I expect your wife would rather enjoy watching the two of you fighting over her.'

He gave her an odd look, curious, amused, almost horrified. 'Women! And they call them the weaker sex! Weak, hell. They're as tough as old boots, and red in tooth and claw.'

'The female of the species is deadlier than the male!' she agreed, smiling at him. 'Well, good luck, Don.' She got out of the car leaving him sitting there, in apparent stupefaction. He was still sitting there when she looked out of her top-floor-flat window but as she stared down he finally started the engine and drove away.

The tree-lined London street was empty then, quiet and tranquil on that May evening, lighted windows along the road, shadows moving on blinds as people walked to and fro in their houses. A wind from the river stirred the leafy branches, the warm air was full of the fragrance of night-scented flowers. From another flat she heard the canned laughter of a TV sitcom; elsewhere somebody was listening to an Italian opera, a tenor singing with passion, a heart-wrenching sound.

That was the last thing she needed—to hear somebody singing about a broken heart. Firmly, Bianca went into the bathroom, ran the taps, poured pink bubble bath into the water and had a long, scented, comforting bath, refusing to think about anything, just letting the strain and tension soak out of her body. It had been an extraordinary twenty-four hours.

Only last night she had been on her way, as she supposed, to have dinner with a stranger whose company they wanted to take over. She had been resigned to a tedious evening, but quite cool and collected.

Then Matt Hearne had had that phone call in his car, and a fast whirl of events had taken her off on a switchback ride from which she was emerging now, the quiet landscape of her life destroyed as if by an earthquake.

She would never be the same again.

She got out of the bath reluctantly and towelled herself, smoothed a musky French after-bath lotion into her skin, so that it turned silky, before putting on a brief blue linen nightdress, with lace at the neck and hem.

She heated a tin of chicken soup and made fingers of toast, then sat down in front of the television to eat, mindlessly watching the news and then a wildlife programme about roe deer on Scottish moorlands.

She was thinking about going to bed when someone tapped on the front door of her flat. Starting, she stood up, hesitating. Who on earth could that be at this hour? Not the student from downstairs again? He was hard to shake off, was always thinking up a new idea for getting into her flat.

Reluctantly she went to the door, opened it on the latch and peered out.

It wasn't the student. It was Matt Hearne.

CHAPTER EIGHT

HER nerves jumped violently. 'How did you get into the building? You didn't ring my bell.'

'That guy from downstairs was going out as I arrived. I said hello to him and he recognised me from the other day, and let me in.'

'I'll have to tell him never to do that again! You could be an axe-murderer, for all he knew! Look, I don't want to talk to you, Mr Hearne. I'm tired. Please go away or I'll call the police!'

'Is Don Heston in there? I didn't see his car outside, but maybe he discreetly parked somewhere else before he joined you?'

She felt herself turning red, and grew even angrier. 'No, he isn't! Please go away. I've got nothing to say to you.'

She began to close the door but he leaned his whole weight on it, keeping it open, the chain stretched to its limit. 'I can talk through the door if you won't open it, but then everyone in this house will hear what I'm saying, and your personal life will be an open secret, won't it?'

How could he guess that she'd hate that? That the very idea of being talked about made her skin creep.

Even angrier now, she bit out, 'Don't try blackmailing me! It won't work. What are you doing here, anyway? Why did you come?'

'Isn't it obvious? You told me Heston was just your

boss, then you went off with him like that. What did you expect me to think?

'Oh, think what you like. I don't care.' She pushed harder on the door, but he put his shoe into the gap.

'Ouch!' he said loudly. 'You're crushing my foot!'

She sensed listening ears in the rest of the building. Suddenly all was silence; no TV playing, no more opera. This was much more exciting—real-life drama being played out yards from their front doors. It was a wonder that they didn't all come out to see what was going on.

'I shall be crippled for life!' Matt mournfully complained.

'Good!' she snapped, hot with temper.

He gave her a reproachful look. 'How can you be so heartless? I've driven all this way, Bianca. You might at least let me in and make me a coffee.'

'You should have stayed with Sara Heston. She'd have given you anything you need—coffee, food.' She paused, added viciously, 'Not to mention her bed for the night, with her in it.'

As soon as she had said that she wished she hadn't. He must have heard the jealousy in her voice and she did not want him to know how primitive her instincts could be.

His eyes narrowed on her face. What was he thinking? She wished she knew.

'Is that what he told you? That Sara and I are having an affair? It isn't true!'

She laughed bitterly. 'Well, you would say that, wouldn't you? You're fighting for your company, you'd use any weapon, and Sara is looking for weapons to use on Don, too. You have a lot in common, in fact. You share the same enemy, and both of you want to hurt him.'

He shook his head soberly. 'Sara is a good woman. I know that's an old-fashioned idea, but believe me, she wouldn't use me…use anyone…as a weapon to hit her husband with!'

She watched him intently, wishing she could believe him. He looked sincere enough, but she had learnt from an early age that men could be deceptive.

'Why should I believe you? Why does Don think she wants a divorce so that she can marry you?'

He looked startled. 'Marry me? That's ridiculous. We're just friends. I haven't even seen that much of her, and when I do see her she is more interested in Lisa than me. She's a motherly woman, not a highly sexed one, I suspect. But her marriage is very important to her—her children, her home, all the things she has spent her life on. Don Heston has hurt her a great deal over the years. Maybe the worm has finally turned. She may want a divorce, but it certainly isn't to marry me.'

'Don thinks she's in love with you. He says she admitted it.'

His face tightened. 'It's a lie. Why should she tell him something like that?'

'Don was far too angry to be lying!'

'This is crazy. Look, we can't go on talking like this, through a crack in a door. Let me in, Bianca.' His voice rose, louder. 'After all, you felt safe enough alone with me last night. I'm still the same guy. You're as safe with me in your flat as you were in my house all night.'

The silence in the rest of the house was deafening now. They must all be holding their breath to make sure they heard everything that was said. They would all be gossiping about her tomorrow. She couldn't risk him saying anything worse. She would have to let him in.

She grimly unhooked the latch, let the door swing open and Matt sauntered coolly past her.

She closed the front door again and gave him an icy stare. 'Don't think you've won! I'm only letting you in because you deliberately tried to embarrass me in front of my neighbours!'

Looking amused and triumphant, he drawled, 'Yes, I noticed they had all gone very quiet. Wouldn't you love to know what they're all thinking right now?'

He gracefully dropped down on to the sofa where she had been eating her soup and toast, brushing that soft brown fall of hair back from his temples, his vivid blue eyes observing the tray which had held the food.

'Smells good, what was it? Soup? Chicken soup? I'd love some. I'm starving.'

'Then go and get yourself a meal somewhere else!' She stayed on her feet, to make it clear that she didn't want him to stay long. 'I shouldn't go back to Sara because Don will be there. He isn't letting go of her without a fight!'

'Glad to hear it. But if he wants a second chance with her, I hope he means to be faithful this time.'

'That's no business of yours!'

'I like Sara, I'd like her to be happy, although God knows why she cares for a man like Heston. But then you like him, too, don't you? Or you wouldn't have driven off with him today. What the hell do women see in him?'

'I keep telling you—there's nothing between me and Don. He's my boss, that's all. I wish you would believe that and stop making nasty remarks.'

'And I wish you would believe me when I say I've

never had an affair with Sara!' He smiled at her, his eyes warm. 'You believe me, and I'll believe you.'

He had a devastating effect on her when he smiled like that. Her pulses went crazy and her mouth dried up. Ever since the first moment she'd seen him he had had this weird effect on her and she resented it. She didn't want to feel like this about the man. About any man! All her life she had been wary of men, keeping them at a distance, afraid to care about them, need them.

When you needed someone you were risking getting hurt. Her mother had been destroyed when her father left. It had ruined her own childhood, maybe even her life. She had adored her father, and he had walked away from her without a second thought, and taught her an indelible lesson.

Looking at Matt with darkened eyes, she knew she dared not let him matter too much. If only she could be sure he hadn't had an affair with Sara Heston.

Had Sara let Don think she had, just to make him jealous? That was female thinking. But she could relate to that. It had certainly worked, hadn't it? Don had been galvanised by the mere suspicion that his wife was in love with another man.

Or was Matt lying to her? Had he let Sara think he would marry her if she divorced Don? Did he have secret plans to do just that?

Matt softly said, 'I hate to tell you this, because you look so sexy, but with that lamp behind you shining through it that nightie is totally transparent.'

She gave a cry of dismay and dashed for her bedroom to put on a dark blue quilted dressing gown which would totally cover her up, but before she could slide into it she heard a sound and looked round to find Matt had followed her, was right behind her, watching.

Flushed and angry, she turned on him. 'Get out of here!'

He was close enough to touch and to her dismay she knew that was what she wanted, knew she ached to touch him. Despite what Don had told her, she couldn't help this fierce, intense attraction to Matt, but she wasn't giving in to it. Her pride and self-respect wouldn't let her.

'Don't come near me!' she burst out, and his eyes darkened, as hard and brilliant as sapphires in the shadowy room.

'I can't help myself, Bianca. That's why I followed you and Heston back to London; I couldn't bear the idea of what might be going on between the two of you.'

'I keep telling you…'

'I know, but I'm jealous of him—you know I am.'

Her heart missed a beat; she was breathless.

'I want you, Bianca,' he said in a low, husky voice, reaching for her, and she wailed in panic.

'No. Don't!' But she was already lost. Matt's hands caught hold of her waist and pulled her close to him, his head came down and his mouth fiercely took hers.

Eyes closing, Bianca saw suns and moons whirling in space; she was dizzy with pleasure and excitement, holding on to his jacket as her head fell back under the hot demand of his kiss. Matt's fingers moved up and down her back, caressing, exploring; she felt his body press intimately, his thigh pushing against her own. She was aching, feverish with desire, her flesh melting into his as she clung, kissing him back.

Matt pushed her backwards step by step, kissing her. She had her arms round his neck, was clasping his head, her mouth hot in surrender.

The backs of her knees suddenly hit the edge of her bed; she swayed and fell backwards, and Matt came down on top of her before she had time to recover. She groaned in satisfaction as she felt him pressing her down on the bed, and arched to meet him.

'I wanted you the minute I saw you,' he muttered, moving on top of her, one hand stroking her bare thigh, the other pushing up her nightdress and caressing her breasts, making her nipples harden and burn.

His mouth descended, his warm tongue sensuously explored her flesh, a slow, tormenting pleasure that kept growing. Her face was buried in his throat. She pressed her open mouth down into his skin, feeling the rapid beat of a blue vein. Matt's life-blood flowing from his heart. She feverishly kissed it, tasted the salt on his hot skin.

He was hurriedly taking off his clothes. She felt the movements, but kept her eyes shut, pretended to be unaware of what he was doing.

She wanted him, her skin taut with desire as his teasing lips opened around a nipple, sucked it slowly into the inner warmth and wetness of his mouth.

Excitement forced a wild cry from her. She had never thought of herself as a sensual woman; she had been too fixed on her career, determined never to lose control, let herself want a man too much.

But now her senses were alive as never before, vibrating, quivering, the heat between her and Matt growing like a forest fire, consuming her, burning her up. She had never felt anything like it in her life. It scared her; it was too much, too soon, too fierce, too hot.

Matt whispered, 'Since Aileen died I haven't even thought about another woman. You're the first and I've been fighting it. After she died, I was sure I'd never fall in love again. I believed all that was over for me. When I realised I was attracted to you I felt so guilty. As if I was betraying Aileen, being unfaithful to her. But it got worse, the more I saw of you; I couldn't keep fighting it. Oh, God, Bianca, I feel like a virgin, as if this was the first time ever. I'm shaking like a leaf—can you feel it?'

Yes, she could feel it; his entire body was trembling. So was hers. She was shaking with passion and need. Open for him, thighs parted, between her thighs a furnace burning.

But he had mentioned his dead wife and she felt as if he had flung icy water over her, put out that fire.

Was that what was really on his mind, in his heart— the woman he had lost, and still mourned, not the woman in his arms now?

Sara Heston wasn't her rival, she realised with a bitter pang. She really believed him now.

Her real rival was Aileen. You couldn't fight a dead woman. Jealousy stabbed deep inside her chest. Her heart ached. He didn't love her. Not the way he had loved his wife.

All he felt for her was desire, a physical need which had nothing to do with the heart. She put her hands against his bare shoulders and shoved him away forcibly.

'No!' She swallowed, took a breath, went on shakily, 'I can't sleep with you, Matt. I don't know what I feel or think, at this moment, but I am certain that it's too soon. We only met a couple of days ago. You're going too fast and I'm scared.'

For a moment he was motionless, then he gave a deep sigh and rolled off her, began to get dressed. Even in her own pain she was aware that his hands were trembling and clumsy.

Huskily he said, 'Okay, you're right, I shouldn't have rushed you. I lost my head; I wanted you so badly I couldn't wait, and I was wrong. Bad timing. I'm sorry.'

The kindness of his voice hurt. She didn't want his kindness. She wanted his love, wanted it more than life itself. It was agony to face the fact that she did not have it.

She sat up, grabbed the duvet and wound it round herself, her head bent to hide her expression.

'Forget it.' Turning the knife in her own chest, she added offhandedly, 'I shall.' And hoped to God he believed her.

A silence. He got up. His voice was rough when he spoke again. 'We have to talk, Bianca. Can I see you tomorrow?'

'Won't you be seeing Sara?'

He sounded angry now. 'Don't start that again! Didn't you hear what I said? I thought you believed me! I swear to you, Sara is a friend, nothing more. Never mind what Don Heston said. I am not having an affair with Sara.'

She knew it now; she believed him. But she was using it as a smokescreen to hide her jealousy of his dead wife. Pretending to be jealous of Sara Heston wasn't shameful. Being jealous of a dead woman was; it would appal him if he knew.

Matt said impatiently, 'I know she's talking of a divorce, but believe me, it isn't on my account. I'm certain she still loves Don, in spite of everything he's done to her. Some women are gluttons for punishment. She's looking after my little girl until I can find a good nanny because Sara loves kids and misses her own while they're away. You have to believe me, Bianca! I suppose you're so used to Don Heston's lies that you think every man you meet is likely to lie.'

'Are you surprised?' she said wearily.

'No, just surprised you've put up with it for so long. If you had any sense you'd quit that job now.'

She spoke the truth in a flat, tired voice. 'Maybe I will. Maybe it is time I left. Once all this is over I shall look for another job and give in my notice.'

'I'm glad about that, anyway.' He watched her silently for a moment, then said gently, 'You're as white as a ghost. Get some sleep, and I'll be back tomorrow morning.' Bending, he kissed her softly on the top of her head, then the door closed and he had gone.

Bianca sank down on the carpet and wept helplessly, her face running with cold tears. All these years, she had been so careful to steer clear of getting involved with any man who could hurt her, might let her down.

Why, why had she fallen in love at last, only to pick a man whose heart was buried with another woman?

CHAPTER NINE

BIANCA was up very early next morning after sleeping badly, her mind obsessed with thoughts of Matt. He would be back, she could be sure of that, and she didn't want to be here when he arrived. She needed time to think about what was happening to her.

You couldn't fall in love in two days. It had to be infatuation, a crazy illusion. It scared her.

Looking at the fine weather outside, she suddenly wanted to get out into the country, away from London. But where should she go? Aunt Susan? she thought. Her mother's cousin was the only relative she still kept in touch with, at a distance. They exchanged Christmas cards and saw each other now and then. Aunt Susan lived on Romney Marsh and never came to London. The journey wasn't easy, which was why Bianca's visits to her were so occasional. You had to take a train from London to Ashford and from there take a slow bus across the marsh.

Luckily, the bus stopped right outside Aunt Susan's cottage, which was close to the beautiful, peaceful church which was the heart of the little village where she lived.

On a day like this it would be a pleasant trip, so Bianca showered, dressed in white jeans and a dark green silk shirt under a white denim jacket, had a quick breakfast of coffee and a yogurt, with some fresh fruit, then left. To save time she decided to take a taxi instead of going by underground to Charing Cross mainline sta-

139

tion. There were usually plenty of taxis passing the end of the road.

As she hovered on the corner, watching the traffic, a car pulled up right next to her. She glanced casually at it, then her heart sank as she recognised the driver.

He leaned over to open the passenger door. She started walking away, fast, but the car kerb-crawled beside her. Matt shouted at her. 'Don't make me get out and chase you, Bianca! Stop playing games and get in the car.'

People were turning to stare. She couldn't get away from him, he would obviously follow wherever she went, so she gave up. Red-faced and furious, she climbed into the front seat, snapping at him, 'Why can't you leave me alone?'

He leaned over her and she stiffened, shrinking down in her seat, voice quivering with alarm. 'What do you think you're doing?'

'Fastening your seat belt,' he said, eyes mocking as he did just that. 'What did you think I was going to do?'

Kiss her, she thought, heart beating far too fast. For one terrifying, wonderful moment she had thought he was about to kiss her, and her body had been electrified.

He smiled and touched her parted mouth with one long, index finger. 'Or can I guess?'

She angrily turned her face away, not answering this deliberate provocation.

He laughed and started his engine again. 'So, where were you off to?'

'Mind your own business.'

'Nowhere special?' he teased. 'Good, then I'll take you for a drive.'

Hurriedly, crossly, she told him, 'I was going to visit

an aunt. She lives miles away, on Romney Marsh. Could you drop me at Charing Cross? I'm going by train.'

'That's okay, I'll drive you there.'

He began to pull out into the traffic again.

She couldn't bear the idea of spending a whole day with him. Already her nerves were jumping, she was shaky from head to toe—after just five minutes!

'It's very kind of you to offer, but I'd much rather you dropped me at Charing Cross.'

Coolly he said, 'I barely know the marsh; it will be interesting to visit it. Does your aunt have a family?'

'Matt, this is crazy!'

He turned his head as they drew up at traffic lights and stared into her eyes, his wide mouth curling in a disturbing mix of mockery and passion.

'Is it? Why? You look very sexy this morning, by the way, in your jeans and that shirt. What a tiny waist you've got.' His eyes lingered on the agitated rise and fall of her breasts in the clinging, silky, open-necked shirt.

Very hot, she said huskily, 'Please, just drop me at Charing Cross.'

'You aren't getting rid of me that easily,' he said. 'Tell me about your aunt.'

She was finding it very hard to think clearly. No man had ever had such a physical impact on her; she fought to control it, force these intense reactions to him out of sight. The last thing she wanted was for him to guess how she felt.

Absently, she said, 'Aunt Susan is nearly eighty and very sweet.'

'You said your mother was dead, didn't you?'

'Did I?' She couldn't remember anything she had

said to him. Those hours in his house in the wild Essex countryside had flashed past. So much had happened to her. She had suffered a bewildering sea change.

'But your father is alive, you said?'

'Yes, he lives in Italy.'

'Works there?'

'Yes. He——' She broke off, the old anger rising inside her again, then forced herself to go on flatly. 'He and my mother were divorced. He married an Italian woman and has a son by her.'

Feeling his intent gaze, she looked away to stare down from Westminster Bridge as they drove over the river to the south side of London. Sunlight glittered on the water; a few barges slowly progressed beneath them. Around them the city lay, towers and spires dwarfed these days by great office blocks which dominated the view.

'Ah,' Matt slowly said.

She looked round at him and the hair rose on her neck. 'What does that mean?' And why was he looking at her like that?

'Do you often see him?'

'No,' she admitted through tight lips, knowing he was guessing at her relationship with her father, and no doubt guessing correctly. Angrily she told him, 'And I don't want to talk about him. So let's drop the subject. What about you? Tell me about your family.'

He gave her a brief, dry glance. 'Oh, you know everything there is to know about me, don't you, Bianca? Your detectives ferreted out every detail of my life from the size of my socks to how many cousins I've got. And, of course, you would have been particularly interested in my family because you would want to buy any shares they had.'

She couldn't deny it and looked away, biting her lip as she faced up to their invasion of his privacy. Who could blame him for being furious? She would hate it if anyone did that to her.

'I'm sorry. I know it must sound ghastly to you, but it was never personal—just business strategy.'

'Don Heston's idea of business strategy! You must get away from that man, you know that, don't you? You won't let yourself be talked into staying?'

'I'll have to find another job first. I can't afford to be without an income, even for a few weeks! I'm not rich, you know.'

'Come and work for me. We need someone like you.'

Her heart jumped at the idea of working with him, but at the same time it frightened her.

'Thanks for the offer,' she slowly said. 'Can I think about it?'

'Take all day!' he ominously said, and her fear intensified.

'Don't pressure me! I've had enough of that badgering from Don!'

They drove through the traffic-clogged, identical grey streets of south London until they finally got on to the motorway heading down to the coast and could speed up.

'Will your aunt be up so early on a Sunday morning?' Matt asked as they drove through Ashford, halfway between London and Folkestone.

'She's always up early. She goes to the early morning service at the church, rain or shine, every Sunday. Her cottage is just across the road; it isn't far to walk.' She was watching the road signs, hurriedly told him, 'We have to turn off here, for the marsh.'

He took no notice, driving on.

'You're going the wrong way!'

'I thought we'd have a look at the sea before we go to your aunt's cottage,' he calmly told her.

She shut her eyes.

'What are you doing?' he asked curiously, watching her.

'Counting to ten.'

'Why?'

'To make sure I really want to hit you before I do!'

He laughed.

'I was not being funny,' she assured him. 'Who do you think you are? First you insist on driving me to Kent when I wanted to take the train; now you're determined to visit the coast before we go to my aunt's place! Will you stop ordering me around?'

'You're very tense,' he merely said. 'You need to unwind, and an hour on the beach will help you do that.'

'Very thoughtful of you, but I would prefer to go straight to my aunt's house, please. Will you take the next turning to the marsh?'

Ignoring her, he mused thoughtfully, 'I love being by a river or at the seaside, don't you? The sound of water, wind in your hair, a feeling of space—it makes you feel great. That's why I bought a house on the Essex estuary. It's such an antidote to London, although it isn't that far to drive. I sail whenever I have time—did I tell you that? You must come out with me some time.'

'Will you listen to me? I do not want to go to the sea, I want to go to my aunt's house!'

'I heard you, Bianca. Are you listening to me?' He turned his head to gaze into her eyes. 'I want to spend the day with you, get to know more about you.'

Her pulses beat fiercely. She looked away, swallowing.

Why am I so afraid? she wondered. Why does it scare me so much to feel like this? Surely I can spend a few hours with the man without shaking like a leaf every time he looks at me or comes close?

'Okay?' he softly asked.

'I was planning to take my aunt out to lunch. She doesn't get out much and she enjoys eating food she hasn't had to cook.'

'I'll get you there before lunchtime,' he promised. 'Tell me more about her.'

With a sigh she faced the fact that she wasn't going to get away from him, so as they drove she talked about Aunt Susan and the tranquil village where she lived.

She was so engrossed that it was a real surprise to her when they drove into the little resort of Dymchurch on the south coast.

'Shall we stop and have some coffee, then take a walk on the beach?' Matt asked.

He parked and they wandered along the narrow, sandy road through the village until they found a café which sold buckets and spades and fishing nets as well as tea or coffee.

It was turning into quite a hot morning so Matt carried their tray outside and they drank their coffee sitting at a red-checked-covered table on the wooden verandah outside the shop. Excited, laughing children ran past down on to the sandy dunes of the beach, disappearing behind the tufts of marram grass.

'I used to come here when I was little,' she told Matt. 'We had summer holidays at a bungalow just down the road and I spent hours every day on this beach.'

'What sort of child were you?'

'Not unlike Lisa, I suppose,' she slowly confessed, struck by the thought. Maybe that was what had drawn her to the child, even before she'd met her? Impulsively, she said, 'She needs to see more of you, you know. I'm sure your mother is very kind to her, but it's you she wants to be with.'

He frowned, looking sharply at her. 'Did she say so?'

'No, she didn't need to. She's a lonely little girl. She needs to see more of you; she misses you when you aren't there, and you don't get down there that often, do you?'

He didn't answer, staring away from her towards the sun-dazzled sea. Was he taking on board what she had said? Or would he ignore her advice?

'Did you miss your father when he left?'

'It upset me, yes.'

'I get the feeling you're still angry with him.'

She shrugged, not wanting to betray too much of herself to him.

'Is that why you've never committed yourself to a man? Because you don't trust them? Because of your father?'

'Don't play the psychologist with me!' She got up angrily and he got up too.

'Okay, let's go for our walk along the beach, then we had better set off for the marsh.'

The beach was full of busy children, building castles, digging holes, playing with big, coloured beach balls. Bianca sat down on the sand and took off her flat shoes and the socks she wore, then rolled up the bottoms of her jeans.

'Good idea,' Matt said, following suit. They hid their shoes and socks behind some marram grass, then, barefoot, they wandered along by the sea, in and out of the water's edge. It was marvellous to feel the cool water flowing over her feet, to hear the soft whisper of the tide as it rolled in from the hazy reaches of the Channel where the heat of the sun was drawing vapour up from the sea and creating a drifting mist.

'On a clear day you can see France,' she told Matt. 'Today you wouldn't guess it was so close or so alike. Same cliffs, same beaches, same countryside. We often took the ferry to spend a day at Boulogne. I expected it to be exotic but it was really much the same.'

'Apart from the food.'

She laughed. 'Yes, French food is better, but I preferred English picnics. The sandwiches seemed nicer to me.' She watched a family with two small children sitting on a tartan rug eating from a wicker hamper. They had packets of sandwiches spread out in front of them.

'Do you like children?' Matt asked.

Truthfully, she admitted, 'I like Lisa. She and I have so much in common.'

Then wished she hadn't said that because it would make him curious, start him asking questions.

But all he said was, 'Yes, I noticed her. She likes you, too; she told me so.'

'Did she?' Bianca was touched.

They skirted a group of children playing very close to the sea. A girl in a tiny bikini threw a ball so hard it sailed over their heads. A boy in bright red shorts leapt sideways in a vain attempt to stop the ball going into the sea.

He crashed into Bianca, who tumbled backwards with a yell.

Matt caught her. The boy fell into the sea, sending up a tidal wave of salt water.

The other children howled with laughter. The boy swam off to get their ball, hurled it back to them and, dripping wet, ran to join in the game.

Bianca found herself in Matt's arms, her face hidden in his shirt. Under her cheek she heard his heart beating. The warmth of his body made her pulse race. Her eyes shut for a moment.

Matt put his face down against her wind-blown hair. 'You okay?'

'Mmm,' she whispered, wanting to stay where she was for ever, held safely in his arms.

'Your hair smells of the sea. Salty and fresh.'

His body had a different scent, musky, intimate. She breathed it in feverishly.

Huskily he said, 'Well, we'd better go, I suppose.'

'Yes,' she said, but neither of them moved, locked in their own private world, until they heard the children behind them giggling.

'Go on, mister, kiss her!'

Matt let his arms drop. Very flushed and breathing fast, he said, 'Come on,' taking her hand.

Bianca stumbled then steadied herself, her heart still knocking violently against her ribs.

They put on their shoes and socks again, climbed back into the car and drove back into Romney Marsh. Neither of them spoke or looked at each other. Those moments on the beach had changed something for her. Maybe for him, too?

When they reached the village she huskily gave Matt directions. He pulled up opposite the beautiful old church and stared at it. Sheep grazed around the gravestones and grass lapped the flint-and-stone walls, with their stained-glass windows, and bell tower.

'Lovely place,' Matt said, and now his voice sounded normal again. She hoped hers would.

'Yes,' she whispered shakily, knowing she sounded as off balance as she felt. 'Let's hope my aunt is in!'

The cottage was tiny—half brick, half white-painted timber, with a tall red-brick chimney at one side of the gabled roof. Wisteria climbed the bottom half of the chimney, and the cottage garden was crowded with roses of every colour, with purple and white lupins and great clumps of marguerite daisies. A white lilac tree spilled shade over the small lawn; a mistle thrush sang from the branches, making Bianca's heart ache. It all looked so tranquil and happy—she wished she felt like that, but how could she after what had happened on the beach?

They walked round to the back of the cottage and peered through the latticed kitchen windows. Aunt Susan was trotting around the small room, intent on making fairy cakes. Dozens of them were cooling on trays on the old deal table in the centre of the white-painted room which looked reassuringly just as it had when Bianca was a child.

She tapped on the glass and the old woman looked round, giving a cry of delighted surprise before hurrying to open the back door.

White-haired, tiny, she folded Bianca into her arms. 'How lovely to see you—why didn't you let me know you were coming? It seems so long since I last saw you!'

Guiltily Bianca apologised. 'I've been meaning to come for ages; I'm sorry not to come more often; time just seems to slip past!'

Grimacing, Aunt Susan said, 'You don't need to tell me that! I still can't believe I'll be eighty soon!' Her eyes flicked past Bianca and widened as she saw Matt.

Bianca introduced him shyly and he shook Aunt Susan's hand, smiling warmly at her.

'I've heard all about you from Bianca; it's very nice to meet you at last.'

Knowing she was very pink, Bianca caught her aunt's fascinated, curious glance.

'It's lovely to meet you, too, Matt,' Aunt Susan said. 'I wish I'd known you were coming, though; I'd have got something special for lunch, but I was just going to have cold meat and a salad. I don't eat much any more; I don't have the same appetite.'

'That's why I didn't ring,' Bianca told her. 'I didn't want you cooking a big lunch for me; I wanted to surprise you and take you out somewhere special for lunch!'

The small, wrinkled face, which had always reminded Bianca of a pansy flower, lit up. 'How exciting! I haven't been out to lunch since the last time you came down.'

'Well, shall we eat in that pub down the road? That was where we went, wasn't it? And they did a great Sunday lunch.'

'That would be lovely, but we had better ring first, to make sure they have a free table; it can get very crowded there on a Sunday. It's the fashion to eat out on Sunday lunchtimes now.' Wiping her hands, Aunt Susan went into her tiny hall to make the call.

'She's wonderful,' Matt said.

'Yes, isn't she?' Bianca moved around the tiny room, staying away from him, feeling now as if he was dynamite which might explode if she got too close.

He was looking at framed photographs on a small table. 'Is this you?' He picked up a small photo of a skinny child in a swimsuit on a beach, all big eyes and long, long legs.

Horrified, she tried to take it from him. 'Don't look at it! I was very plain.'

'You were sweet,' he protested.

Aunt Susan came back beaming. They were lucky; a table was free in the small dining room of the eighteenth-century pub. Matt drove them there. Neither he nor Bianca said much, but Aunt Susan talked a blue streak, about the vicar, the village gardening club, her problems with ground elder and the exciting events that year of the local women's institute.

Clearly Aunt Susan had more friends than she did, Bianca reflected enviously, and led a much busier social life, but then living in a small community probably meant that you had to create your own fun; it wasn't laid on for you, as it was in London, with its theatres and cinemas.

As they ate potted shrimps with toast her aunt asked her, 'Have you heard from your father lately?'

'A postcard the other day, but it didn't say much.'

'Still, he was thinking of you.'

Bianca smiled bleakly. 'His new family is all he cares about. He only remembered me because it was his son's birthday and that reminded him of me.'

She became aware then of Matt's narrowed gaze and looked down at the table, flushed and self-conscious.

She didn't want to talk about this in front of him, but before she could change the subject Aunt Susan said gently, 'Well, doesn't that tell you that he does think about you? You're still his daughter, Bianca, he misses you. Have you been to Italy to see him and meet his wife and the little boy?'

'No,' she tightly said, still not looking up.

'That's very sad, Bianca—I think you should go over there. You only ever have one father, you know.'

'He left my mother, and me, we didn't leave him,' Bianca obstinately said, her face clenched in anger.

'I was fond of your mother, but she was never a very happy woman. The marriage didn't work. They weren't suited, and it wasn't all your father's fault. In fact, I had a lot of sympathy for your father. He really tried, but in the end he had to face the fact that the marriage was a failure, so he had the courage to go.'

Although she didn't look in his direction Bianca knew Matt was listening intently and she hated the thought of what he was learning.

'I don't want to talk about this, Aunt Susan! Can we change the subject?'

Aunt Susan looked sadly at her and Bianca felt ashamed for having snapped like that. Her aunt meant well. If only she hadn't chosen to talk about the past in front of Matt!

Their main course, the roast of the day, lamb with mint sauce and fresh garden peas, arrived, in time to break up the tension.

They followed that with a delicious pudding, then coffee, drunk in a leisurely way in the garden of the pub, with Matt telling Aunt Susan all about his own home, in the Essex marshes.

An hour later they dropped Aunt Susan back at her cottage. Matt tactfully stayed in the car while Bianca walked her aunt through the garden to her front door.

'What a very nice man,' Aunt Susan said, with one of her sharp, quick glances. 'Am I right in guessing it's serious?'

Very flushed, Bianca protested, 'I only just met him!'

Her aunt smiled. 'All right, I won't ask any more questions. And I'm sorry I upset you by talking about your father.'

'No, I'm sorry I got so uptight,' Bianca protested. 'I shouldn't have got so cross. It all happened a long time ago and I'm a big girl now. It was nice to see you, Aunt Susan. I'll try to get down again soon.'

'And bring that lovely man with you!'

Bianca didn't answer that. She hugged her aunt, then hurried back to the car and got in beside Matt, waved until Aunt Susan's small, dignified figure vanished into the distance.

The journey back to London took over two hours. Matt parked and looked down at her, his eyes searching her face as if for clues to her hidden feelings.

'Have dinner with me tonight.'

She shook her head. 'Thank you, but I'm expecting some important business calls, and I have some work to do, too.'

'That man works you too hard. The sooner you get away from him the better.'

'Don't start that again!'

'Okay, I'll leave it till tomorrow.'

'I may be busy tomorrow, too.'

His eyes were fixed, intense. 'Bianca, don't think I'll give up or go away—I won't. This is important—I know it, you know it.'

Her heart turned over and over like a fish being landed in a net. She opened the car door, not looking at him.

'Sorry, I must rush.'

'Tomorrow! I'll pick you up here at seven,' he shouted as she slammed the door shut and fled.

Back in her flat she sat down before her legs collapsed under her. Her head was filled with images of him: his floppy, silky hair that shone in sunlight like gold, his bright, mocking blue eyes, that smile that made her pulse race.

She wanted badly to be in his arms, to touch him, kiss him. The memory of those moments on the beach made her weak. Matt Hearne was destroying her peace of mind. But she was afraid to give in to how she felt. It could be an illusion, a momentary impulse—on his side or on hers. It had happened too fast; it couldn't be real, couldn't last.

Next day she was up at the crack of dawn and went into the office as usual, although she was tempted to hide in her flat, but it was safer at the office. Matt could hardly force his way in there; she had a room full of staff between herself and unwanted visitors.

There was a message from Don on her office answering machine. 'Hi, Bianca. I'm finally off to Australia in a couple of hours.' A pause, then he added, 'Taking my wife with me.'

Bianca's jaw dropped. What had he said?

He laughed and she had the feeling someone else laughed, in the background—Sara? Or was she imagining it? It had certainly sounded like a woman's laughter, breathy, soft.

'I bet that made you jump!' Don added. 'Yes, I'm taking Sara. Remind me to give you a raise when I get back. You were right. I owe you one, Bianca.'

She smiled. 'You're entirely welcome, Don,' she said, aloud, even though he could not hear her.

'Oh,' he went on, 'and drop the take-over.'

She gasped in disbelief.

'I promised Sara I would leave Matt Hearne alone,' Don said. 'It seems she was very fond of his wife, and is very taken with his kid, too. She's managed to find a nanny to take care of the little girl, by the way; no problem there. We're going to wander around Australia after I've finished my business meetings, getting to know each other again. So I'm not sure when I'll be back.'

A pause, then she distinctly heard someone else whispering. Don sighed. 'Oh, yes, and Sara wants me to tell you that it was me who told young Mistell that...well, I let him think that...there was something going on between you and me. That's why he ended it with you.'

She wasn't entirely incredulous although she had never wanted to believe Don would go so far as to lie to Harry. Sitting at her desk, pale and tense, she thought, How could he do that? Anger surged through her.

Sounding chastened and uneasy, Don went on, 'I'm sorry, Bianca. It was a rotten thing to do. But I was afraid you would leave if you married Mistell, and you're one of my most valued executives; I didn't want to lose you.'

The flattery did not soften her anger, nor did it quite ring true. He was talking about her as a colleague to disguise his real motive from his wife, who was listening. He wouldn't want Sara to know he had broken up her affair with Harry Mistell in the hope of getting her for himself. She wished this was not a recorded message, that she could tell Don just what she thought of him.

Hurriedly Don said, 'And honestly, I didn't think you were serious about him; I was sure you weren't in love, and wouldn't get hurt. I wouldn't have done it if I'd thought you cared about him.'

The whispering was audible again; his wife was scolding him.

He sighed. 'No excuse, I know. Look, why don't you

write to him, tell him I lied? Tell him he can thump me when I get back.'

She wouldn't do that, of course. Whatever might have happened between her and Harry was dead long ago. You couldn't rekindle a flickering flame once it went out. It had never been very deep or very important, anyway. The way she now felt about Matt had taught her how little Harry had really meant to her.

'Sorry, Bianca,' Don said with obvious relief. 'We've got to go. See you when I see you—which may be a month or more!'

The message clicked off; there were others following it, but Bianca listened to Don's message again to take in everything he had said.

Yes, Sara had been listening while he made the call. Don had got his wife back, and sounded over the moon about that—but what had she told him about her relationship with Matt?

What was the truth about them? Was Matt lying—or had Sara lied when she'd told her husband that she wanted a divorce so that she could marry Matt? Why would she do that, if it wasn't true?

Bianca wished she knew exactly what their relationship had been. Had they been lovers? Well, Sara had made her choice now, and whatever had been going on between her and Matt was over.

There was no point in thinking about it; it was nothing to do with her, Bianca thought grimly. Except... how could she stop?

How did you shut off your mind, drown the jealousy and pain she had been feeling ever since Don told her his wife wanted a divorce to marry Matt?

Suddenly she stiffened, hearing his voice on the tape.

Why did she feel he was making love to her whenever he spoke to her with that soft, sensual intonation?

'I've just been to your nest again, and found the bird had already flown. My God, you get up early. I'm presuming you've gone to work. I've tried ringing you there but the operator keeps telling me you aren't taking any calls. Pick you up tonight, at your place, seven o'clock? I'll book dinner somewhere very special. See you.'

Bianca sat staring out of the window at the pigeons, strutting on the grey-blue tiles which were strangely close in shade to their colouring, except that in the May sunlight, as they moved, their wings were iridescent, shimmering and changing through the spectrum, phosphorescent-green, slate-blue and rose-pink.

The sound of his voice made her heart sing, but she was still afraid. When he'd begun making love to her in her bedroom the other night she had lost control within seconds; had been going crazy, burning up with desire as he touched her.

She wanted him now, in the cold light of day, in her office, sitting at her desk. It wasn't necessary to have moonlight, or music, or for her to have been drinking wine... The desire she felt was constant, instinctive, deep.

If he walked in at this second she wouldn't be able to resist him. Ever since she'd first set eyes on him she had wanted to touch him, had ached to make love to him.

Her temples pulsed; was she getting a migraine? She put her elbows on her desk and bowed her head into her hands, pressing her palms into her eyes, shutting out the bright May light, and trying to make herself stop thinking.

Monday was usually a nice, quiet day, but luckily, today, she had to deal with the ramifications of ending the Hearne take-over, file all the documents, tag off the files on their computers, tell everybody who had been working on it to switch to something else. She was kept too busy to have time for anything else.

On her way home that evening she saw an advertisement for Italian holidays in her newspaper, and found herself wondering what her father's Italian wife was really like, and whether her half-brother, Lorenzo, was all Italian, took after his father, or was a mixture of both his parents.

It was odd to think she had a half-brother in the world and knew almost nothing about him.

Maybe Aunt Susan was right? Maybe it was time to bury the past, go to Lake Como, meet Maria and her little boy?

Would it be a betrayal of her mother if she did? Her mother had been very bitter when the marriage broke up. She had died bitter; her life had been very unhappy for years.

As Bianca let herself into her flat she realised that she had been hating and resenting her father all these years not because of what he had done to her mother, at all, as she had always told herself—but because of what he had done to her, because of the misery of her childhood with an angry, unhappy woman, not to mention her own pain and jealousy. Her father had left a dark shadow over her whole life ever since.

She had never trusted any man because her father had deserted her, she admitted. Her emotional life had been a desert. She had never even been able to fall in love with Harry, much as she had liked him.

But something had happened inside her lately, over

this past week. She had changed; she wasn't quite sure how. She knew why, though.

It was a very warm evening; she was perspiring, her heartbeat erratic; she poured herself a cold drink from the fridge—some sparkling mineral water—drank half of the glass at once, then went into her bathroom to have a shower.

Cooler, her heartbeat slower, she chose a white linen dress from her wardrobe and got dressed, keeping an eye on her watch. Matt had said he would be here at seven. She wanted to be calm and at ease, not at all flurried or agitated, when he arrived.

Glancing at her watch, she saw it was nearly seven now, and at once her heart speeded up, her mouth went dry.

She finished her glass of sparkling water standing by the window, watching for his car, but he hadn't shown up by ten past seven.

It was then that she suddenly noticed a light on her answering machine, telling her she had a message.

She quickly went over to play the tape back and heard Matt's curt, cold voice, with a jump of alarm.

'Sorry, Bianca, I can't make it this evening. I'll be in touch as soon as I can. See you.'

That was it. His voice ended as abruptly as it had begun. The machine switched off. She stood staring at it, going white, her stomach clenched in pain and shock.

He hadn't even bothered to make an excuse; the apology had been brusque and offhand.

A groan broke out of her. God, what a fool she had been! He had been using her. All she had been to him was a weapon to help him fight off the TTO take-over. Matt had turned on his considerable sex appeal, his seductive charm, and she had fallen for it, hook, line and sinker.

How could she have been so taken in?

She had thought she was cool-headed and shrewd, able to cope with any line a man tried to spin her. Yet Matt had had no trouble fooling her. In just a couple of days he had managed to undermine all her defences; he had got to her, really got to her.

But now Don had dropped the take-over bid, and Matt knew he didn't have to bother to pretend any more.

So he was dumping her.

CHAPTER TEN

THAT evening she rang her father who was audibly amazed to hear from her, not surprisingly, because she couldn't remember ever ringing him before.

'Is something wrong, Bianca?'

'No, no,' she disclaimed, her voice shy. 'It's just that...I was thinking of coming to your part of Italy and...I thought...well, I might visit you while I'm there. I shall stay at a hotel, of course, but it seems a pity to miss the chance to meet up.'

Luke Milne exclaimed in surprise. 'You're coming here?' He paused, as if taking in the idea, then began throwing excited questions at her. 'Why didn't you let us know sooner? Are you coming alone, or with a tour group? Are you touring the lakes, or just staying at Lake Como? How long will you be here?'

In the background a woman's voice began talking in excited, rapid, mellifluous Italian. Was that Maria? Bianca wished she understood what she was saying— was Maria horrified by the prospect of an unknown stepdaughter appearing on the doorstep?

'*Sì, sì,*' her father said. '*Certo.*' Then, in English, he said to Bianca, 'Maria wants me to tell you she is thrilled to hear you're coming at last. She says you must stay with us; there is a lovely room for you, with a wonderful view of the lake and the mountains; you will be far more comfortable there than staying in a hotel. And Lorenzo will be very happy to meet his big sister.'

The words had an odd effect on her—it hadn't really

sunk in until that moment that she had a half-brother. Oh, of course she had known, but she hadn't felt it, hadn't thought about being a little boy's older sister. Her resentment of her father's second marriage and second family had stopped her from seeing things from the little boy's point of view. He must be curious about her. Any child would be, if told he had an unknown, older sibling.

She wouldn't want to hurt the child. Suddenly she was curious about him. Did he look like their father? Maybe he even looked like her? That was a strange thought, the possibility that there was some family resemblance. Blood ties were funny things.

Impulsively, she said, 'I'm looking forward to getting to know him, too,' and knew it was true. Her feelings had changed; she wanted to see this half-brother whose existence she had ignored for eight years. She wished she hadn't. 'And it's very kind of Maria to offer me a room, but really, I could go to a hotel.'

'No, no, we would love to have you stay with us, then Maria can see a lot of you and really get to know you.'

'Well, if you're quite sure...'

'Maria wants you to meet her family; they would think it very strange if you stayed in a hotel. Italians are very family-orientated.'

'Does she have many relatives nearby?' Bianca wasn't sure she wanted to face a large Italian tribe who might be resentful of her long estrangement from her father and the way she had ignored Maria.

'Yes, hers is a big family.'

'Well...thank you, as long as I won't be a nuisance.' She hesitated, thinking that it could be embarrassing if she found Maria was secretly hostile and hiding it from

Luke Milne. This was very much an unknown situation she was entering into.

'Nuisance? Not at all. Maria is very hospitable. When will you be arriving? Are you flying?'

'Yes, to Milan, but then I'll get a coach to Lake Como.'

'No, no, you don't want to take the coach—I'll pick you up at the airport. Give me the date and time of your flight and I'll be there.'

She didn't hear a word from Matt that week, and as she flew to Italy the following weekend she was on edge. She had barely seen her father since she was a very young child—they were virtual strangers; how would they be able to talk to each other?

All her life she had been filled with bitterness towards the man she was soon to see again; she knew she couldn't even have contemplated visiting him five, ten years ago, even just a year back—but something inside her had changed lately.

She wasn't sure what had happened, only that the ice which had been packed around her heart had cracked and she felt very differently about her father. She was very curious, too, about the woman who had replaced her mother in her father's life—and she was actually looking forward to meeting their son, Lorenzo, whom she had resented from the minute she heard of his birth, but now, amazingly, was eager to see.

A revolution had happened inside her heart; she didn't know why.

Staring out of the plane window at the white clouds through which they were descending towards Como, she grimaced.

Of course she knew why! She had met Matt.

It was that simple. The instant she saw him had been

like a violent earthquake, and that moment had been followed in quick succession by a whole series of aftershocks which weren't over yet, which still reverberated inside her.

Love altered everything. She was different; the way she saw her life was new. Her feelings were bewildering, confused, intense, and so new to her that she was having trouble recognising or understanding them.

The plane landed smoothly. She followed the other passengers through the terminal, collected her suitcase and walked out through the barrier to find her father waiting for her. For a second or so they stared at each other uncertainly, then Luke Milne flung his arms around her and hugged her tightly, kissing her on both cheeks. 'Bianca! You're really here; I don't believe it! I kept thinking you wouldn't be on the plane, you wouldn't come. I'm so happy to see you.'

He had aged—but then what had she expected? She absorbed the change in him—he was fatter than he had been, had a large stomach, his hair was thinner, greyer, was sliding back off his forehead, leaving a bald patch at the front. His face was fuller, very tanned and lined. She only just recognised him.

He held her arms and stepped back to stare at her. 'I only just recognised you—it had to be you; you were the only blonde in sight. But you're so grown up. I always think of you as a teenager with a blonde ponytail and skin-tight jeans.'

'That was a long time ago,' she said, wistfully.

'Yes.' Her father sighed. 'Well, give me your luggage.' He took her case firmly out of her grip. 'Did you have a good flight?'

'Yes, it was fine.' She followed him through the throng of departing travellers, thinking that if he had not greeted her first she might never have picked him out of the crowd. They were strangers to each other. Wasn't that sad?

'I hate flying; I prefer to take the train,' Luke Milne said over his shoulder, grimacing.

'Are Maria and Lorenzo waiting at home?' she asked as she got into his red Fiat, parked in the airport car park.

He nodded. 'Yes, Maria said I should come alone, to give us a chance to talk to each other alone. We have a lot of catching up to do, she said.'

That had been thoughtful. She was becoming very curious about this unknown stepmother whom she had hated for so long.

Her father drove like all the other Italians on the motorway—very fast, zipping in and out of the traffic, hooting all the time, talking to her, gesticulating, laughing.

She watched him and found no resemblance to the man she had known. This contented, demonstrative man wasn't the father she vaguely remembered, but she liked him. He was far more Italian than he had been in her childhood. She couldn't remember him seeming different from the English fathers of other children. He had spoken English without an accent, moved and reacted like an Englishman—but obviously the Italian side which he had inherited from his mother had been present all the time, out of sight, sunk down into his nature.

When he'd started living in Italy that half of him had risen to the surface. His Italian was natural and fluent, after these years away from England; he had soaked up the atmosphere around him, used his hands and shoulders while he talked, laughed all the time, was so much more relaxed and lively.

Had he ever loved her mother? she wanted to ask him, but was too shy to put the question into words. When had he stopped loving her? Why had their marriage failed? Whose fault had it been? His—or her mother's?

She had always assumed it to be his, but Aunt Susan had taken a tolerant view—she must have known them both well. She had seemed to think there were faults on both sides. Their marriage had just been one of those mistakes people made, blindly plunging into a future they couldn't see, taking mere liking for love, getting married before they really knew each other well enough to understand what they were getting into.

Had her mother loved him? Bianca had no idea, although she vividly remembered how bitter her mother had been after he left. She had got rid of every memory of him, everything he had owned; she'd burnt piles on a bonfire in the back garden—clothes, books, every photo in which he appeared—and she'd never mentioned him after that. He was wiped out of their lives for good.

It had been typical behaviour—her mother had been a determined woman, tough-minded, even hard, rather cold, full of silent resentment towards her ex-husband and life itself.

She had never married again but she had not been happy, either. Bianca had always assumed her mother had been badly hurt, but now she wondered—would it have made any difference if her father had stayed? Had her mother always been a reserved, cold woman?

Looking back to her earliest years, she couldn't remember her mother being any different. Was that really why the marriage had broken up? If she got the chance later, she would take the risk of asking her father some questions about the past. Her mother had always refused to talk about him, but perhaps he would be prepared to discuss the past.

They arrived at Bellagio after a long and tiring drive. The little town rose up on narrow, winding roads built in steps from the lakeside, the white walls of small houses on each side bright with red geraniums and blue lobelia, and shops selling shoes, clothes, hats, groceries—everything you could want from the look of their windows—scattered here and there all the way up to the top.

'Don't worry, you won't have to walk up the steps; we live further along the lake on flat land,' her father laughingly explained as he saw her glance up the steep lanes they drove past in some apprehension.

'That's a relief! It must be a problem, if you're old, climbing up there several times a day!'

'Not if you're used to it.' He was concentrating on the lakeside road ahead. Bianca stared at the reflections on the surface of the calm water—blue sky, the mountains towering around the lake, the trees and flowering shrubs you saw in every garden. She wished she had brought her camera—maybe she could buy one somewhere? Photos you took yourself brought back far more memories than postcards or pictures in books.

Especially if you had people in your photos.

'Here we are,' Luke Milne said, pulling up, and she sat straight in the seat, staring in a daze, hardly believing what she saw. The house was a dream.

Square, detached, the pink stucco house stood in a garden which took the breath away. A riot of colours in all shades of pink, red, purple and yellow, it was crammed with thirty-foot-high camellias whose blooms were like great saucers, delicate, foaming azaleas and rhododendrons which grew even larger, some of them spreading ten feet wide and forty feet high.

She had never seen anything like them. They grew around the house, half-hiding it, dwarfing it, so that it looked like a doll's house from the front, although as she counted the sash windows she worked out that there had to be four bedrooms.

White-painted trellis was fixed all over the walls, dripping with the star-like flowers of pink-and-white clematis. Each upper window had a balcony with elaborate white scroll ironwork through which one saw pots of salmon-pink geraniums standing on the balcony floor, the branches tumbling down into the air, heavy with blossom.

Her father parked on a small tiled strip at one side of the garden, watching her rapt face. When he got out of the car Bianca got out, too, walked with him to the front door, too enchanted to speak.

Looking at her sideways, her father gave a satisfied smile. 'You like it?'

'It's beautiful,' she breathed. 'Are you the gardener, or is it Maria?'

'We share the work—indoors and out. That's how our marriage works.'

'I can see you're very happy with her. Happier than you were with Mum?'

He sighed. 'I don't want to say anything against your mother, Bianca. But our marriage didn't really work after the first year or two. It wasn't her fault. We just weren't suited. I fell out of love, and then realised I didn't even like her very much. I was unhappy for quite a while before I left. It seemed stupid to go on; I had to get away. The only reason I stayed as long as I did was you. I didn't want to hurt you, and I'm sorry that I did, Bianca. That's my only regret.'

She was silent, not knowing what to say for a minute, then she changed the subject. 'I always thought you left us for Maria.'

'No, I hadn't even met her then. I met her after moving here. Your mother had divorced me by then, I was free, so we got married at once. Our marriage has been perfect. We learn from each other. She taught me to cook, I taught her to garden, we work together all day, talking, singing. We're a noisy family, I'm afraid, but our neighbours aren't close enough to want to complain. And here she is! She saw us arriving.'

The front door had opened. Suddenly stricken with shyness, Bianca took in a large, plump woman with thick, gleaming black hair plaited and wound on top of her head in a coronet, golden, glowing skin, and big black eyes which smiled as Maria opened her arms to her.

'At last you're here!' she said in English, hugging Bianca as if quite unaware of her stepdaughter's faltering, uncertain reserve, the stiffness of her body in that warm embrace. 'I am so glad to see you, *cara*.' To prove it, she kissed Bianca on both cheeks. 'You have made your father very happy. And me, too! Now we are a family!'

Reaching round behind herself, she pulled forward a struggling boy, slender as a faun, with pointy pink ears and a delicate face. 'This is Lorenzo. Lorenzo, kiss your sister.'

He took after his mother more than his father, thought Bianca, staring down at him. Black hair, black eyes, an olive complexion and that slight, graceful build which in his mother had become full and stately.

Bianca bent down and kissed him on both cheeks. *'Ciao, Lorenzo.'*

'Ciao,' he muttered, eyeing her, then, half-accusingly, in Italian, said, 'Mama, you said she would look like me! But she doesn't! She's a blonde.'

Laughing, Bianca said, *'Scusi, Lorenzo.'* She was glad she had brushed up on her Italian. Although he and his mother spoke English, Bianca wanted to talk to them in their own language as much as possible.

The next few days were hectic. Bianca met so many relatives she found it hard to remember names or faces, but the warmth of the welcome from all of them lifted her spirits, made her feel very much at home, as Maria and her father wished.

Her father and Maria were always busy in the kitchen, cooking for lunch or dinner, when they were not gardening or tidying the house.

Every morning Bianca got herself coffee and some rolls and black cherry jam Maria told her she always made herself from the cherry trees in the back garden. Their blossom was just fading, turning brown, dropping from the branches, littering the grass beneath them, like melting confetti.

She got into the habit of eating a leisurely breakfast at a wooden table under the trees, breathing in the incredible perfume of all the flowers. She needed time alone to absorb so many new discoveries.

Lorenzo was a charming, lively, funny little boy. Within a few hours of arriving, Bianca was very fond of him, and of his mother. All these years, Bianca had imagined that Maria hated her and wanted to keep her out of her father's life, but she soon realised how wrong she had been. Maria was delighted to welcome her into this small family group; she was used to an extended family; it was natural to her, and she had a warm and loving heart which eagerly made room for one more.

After breakfast she usually helped Maria prepare the vegetables for lunch, and, after that, she liked to take a stroll along the lakeside.

'Anything I can get you, Maria?' she asked on the fifth morning of her stay with them.

'No, thank you, Bianca. The sun is very hot, remember. Put on a hat.'

Smiling, Bianca put on a cream straw hat her father had bought her the day after she arrived, insisting that she wear it whenever she went out; it had a broad brim from which a blue satin ribbon fluttered at the back.

Although she usually wore it, she was still acquiring quite a tan after a week here. Her face was a smooth, golden brown; her blonde hair was so bleached by the sun that it was almost silvery. She was afraid she was putting on weight after all the terrific food Maria kept serving up at the table, but so far it didn't show much. Her slim figure looked very good in the clinging yellow cotton T-shirt which was cut off at her midriff, and the sky-blue brief shorts which ended at her upper thighs, revealing long, tanned legs.

She got lots of stares as she strolled along the lakeside, but she was too busy gazing at the scenery to take any notice of the men she passed.

The lake had a dreamy distance, shades of blue fading one into another in the sky, stretching off to infinity, while the milky, tranquil water lapped gently at the wooden landing stages and banks beside which she walked. It was going to be another perfect day; Maria was right—it would be very hot later. Maybe later she would catch the ferry up to Como itself—she hadn't done so yet, but she planned to, before she left.

She sat at a table on a café terrace, her straw hat shading her face, feeling lazy and contented, and drank iced tea while she wrote a postcard to Aunt Susan.

Someone halted beside her, a dark shadow falling across her body, and she looked up.

Her heart stopped. Started again, dangerously fast.

It was Matt.

CHAPTER ELEVEN

'WHAT are you doing here?' she burst out, so dazed she might almost have believed him if he claimed it was pure coincidence.

'Looking for you.' He gave her that old, charming smile, but she resisted its dazzling allure, her green eyes cold, her face hostile.

'You flew to Italy just to see me? I don't believe it—I suppose the truth is you are really here on business? Are you mixing business with pleasure, Mr Hearne?' A thought occurred to her—it should have occurred before but she had been too shaken by seeing him for her brain to be working efficiently. 'How did you know I was in Italy?'

'I went to your office, your secretary told me you were on holiday; I asked her where and she told me.'

'She shouldn't have done!' But it hadn't occurred to her to warn Patricia against Matt Hearne. She had not expected him to turn up in person. Faced with his looks and charm, Patricia wouldn't have been able to resist, even if she had been warned against him.

'I talked her into telling me,' he drawled with amusement. 'Don't blame her; I told her it was vital I spoke to you.'

'She should have rung me to check!'

The waiter had wandered out from the café, expecting Matt to order something. Hearing them speaking in English, he said, 'Yes, please, sir?'

Matt half turned, smiled at him, spoke in Italian, surprising her again. How many languages did he speak?

Not that it should surprise her to discover he spoke other languages. He was a businessman with a growing company. If he wanted to sell his product across Europe he would need to be a linguist.

While he was distracted, she pulled herself together, got to her feet, gathered up her postcards and purse, and dropped some coins on top of the bill the waiter had left on the table when he had brought her coffee. She started to walk very fast back towards her father's home, but Matt caught up with her a moment later.

'Running away again?'

Without looking at him she curtly said, 'The take-over has been abandoned, you don't have anything more to worry about. You and I have nothing to say to each other. I don't know what you're doing here.'

'Oh, yes, you do! I had to see you.'

'Why? Your only interest in me was the hope of blocking our take-over, but you don't need to worry about that any more.' She tried to sound indifferent, as if she couldn't care less, but couldn't keep a bitter sting out of her voice as she said, 'You made that crystal-clear when you broke our dinner date and then never rang again.'

Glancing sideways at her from under his lashes, he quietly said, 'I couldn't make it to dinner that night because my mother had just had a heart attack.'

She looked up in shock and met his darkened blue eyes. 'Oh, I'm sorry—how is she now?'

'In a convalescent home just outside London, recovering slowly. It wasn't, thank God, a major attack; the doctors think it was caused by the stress of the operation.'

'It must have been a traumatic experience for her at her age! Operations are a set-back for anyone, but for anyone older it is far worse.'

'Yes, and the anaesthetic used can have an effect on the heart. They had said they were worried about her heart, but they thought she had weathered the operation safely. Thank heavens she was in hospital when she had the attack, so she got medical attention immediately, but I must admit it scared me stiff. I only heard about it just before I was leaving to pick you up.'

'So that's why you were so curt on the phone,' she thought aloud.

'Was I?' He grimaced. 'Sorry. I was so anxious I hardly remember what I said to you; I was just desperate to get to the hospital as soon as possible.'

'You must have been very worried.' She slowed her pace, and he fell into step, strolling beside her, walking so close their arms brushed now and then.

Her skin shivered at the warm contact with him. Out of the corner of her eyes she took in what he was wearing. Pale blue cotton trousers and a short-sleeved dark blue T-shirt which left his brown throat and forearms bare, so that she could see the faint golden hairs sprinkled all over his skin. In this intense sunlight his light brown hair had a golden shimmer, like a halo around his head.

He turned his head to look down into her green eyes. 'Did you think I had lost interest in you because the take-over wasn't going to happen, Bianca?'

She flushed, realising she had given herself away. How could she pretend to be indifferent to him now? 'What else was I to think? Especially when you didn't ring back.'

'I'm sorry,' he said gently. 'My mother was so ill I

stayed at the hospital most of the next two days; I was so afraid to leave her I didn't even eat, and then when she was better I went down to get Lisa and bring her to London. I've decided to sell the house in Essex and buy a house somewhere close to London. You made me see it was time we got to know each other better, so from now on she'll live with me. I'll get a nanny to help out, but I'll spend as much time as I can with her. She's here with me, now.'

Startled, she looked around. 'Here? Where is she?'

'I left her at your father's house—his wife insisted on feeding her; she decided Lisa looked hungry.'

Bianca laughed. 'Yes, that sounds like Maria!'

'They told me you were here by the lake.'

Crossly, she snapped, 'I wish you hadn't gone there! They'll be imagining all sorts of things!'

'Nothing that isn't true, Bianca,' he softly said, and her skin heated at the intimate look in those amazing blue eyes.

'Don't play games with me, Mr Hearne!'

She broke into a run, her long, tanned legs loping fast, and a moment later was back at the house. A glance over her shoulder told her that Matt wasn't far behind her, so she dived into one of the secret alcoves in the garden. He wouldn't find her there; she would have a few minutes to herself before going to see Lisa.

In this little bower she was out of sight of the windows, but not entirely out of earshot, because she heard Lisa chattering away to Maria in the kitchen and was moved by the childish voice.

Lisa must be so excited, going on holiday with her father, alone. What was she saying to Maria? They would be dying of curiosity.

They had dropped hints, asking if there was a man

in her life, and she had lied, told them that there wasn't. Of course, in one sense that had been true. Matt wasn't part of her life; she had known him for a few days, that was all, and whatever had briefly been between them had ended the day he'd rung to tell her in that terse way that he couldn't take her to dinner. When he'd never rung again, leaving her suspended in limbo, it had hurt badly.

She stared into a huge purple rhododendron, seeing dew still trembling on the golden inner heart. Why had she reacted with such anger and anguish to a broken date? Why were her feelings in such turmoil even now she knew why Matt had broken their date and failed to ring her for days?

She had felt just like that when her father had walked out on her and her mother, she remembered, looking back down the years to her childhood.

That couldn't have anything to do with how she felt now, though. She was an adult; a woman, not a child.

Or had that first rejection and betrayal set a pattern? Had she got Matt mixed up with her father in her head? A heavy cold pang thudded inside her chest.

Yes, maybe that could explain a lot.

Her father had vanished without explanation when she was too young to understand why—and she had never got over it; she had never trusted men since. For years she had pursued her career and refused to get involved with any of the men who tried to date her. Even poor Harry, whom she had liked so much—she had never reached the point of letting herself care deeply even about him. Love was too much of a risk.

Somehow Matt had broken through her defences. She had begun to believe she could trust him, had risked letting herself warily, tentatively, start to love him.

And when Matt had walked out on her, too, the pain she had felt was intensified by all the unresolved hurt of losing her father.

Was that it? She could read a balance sheet, could understand how a complex company worked—but she found it hard to read her own heart.

The wind blew from the lake again and white petals from a camellia blew down over her; she absently brushed them from her shorts and the long, tanned legs.

A movement made her start violently, looking up. He had found her.

'I went into the house but they said you hadn't come back yet,' he said, brushing his hand across her blonde hair. 'You look as if you've just got married. There's white confetti all over your head.'

Trembling at the touch of his hand, she said, 'The wind blew down petals from the camellia.'

His blue eyes wandered over the half-revealed pale gold of her arms and legs, the deep curve of her breasts, her bare throat, usually so pale, but given a lovely colour by the sun here at Lake Como this week.

She felt her nipples hardening and hoped he couldn't see the rounding of her breasts under the T-shirt.

Matt sat down on the stone seat next to her, stretching his long legs out with a sigh.

'I must be out of condition—I'm out of breath after doing all that walking, and my pulse is going far too fast.' He reached out a hand to take hold of one of hers. 'Feel,' he said, and put her fingers on his neck, pressing them down into his skin above an artery.

Her pulse picked up his and beat rapidly in unison. She hurriedly pulled free, trembling, staring at the grass around them.

Matt took hold of her chin and pulled her round to

face him. 'Stop running away, Bianca. What are you so scared of? Me? Or yourself?'

Her green eyes looked into his blue ones; the intensity of his stare made her draw breath audibly, her own eyes shifting away, unable to hold that look. 'Don't!'

'Don't what?'

'Look at me that way.'

'You're beautiful; I can't see enough of you.' He ran one finger down her face, from her temples, over her eyelids, brushing her lashes, along her warm cheek to her mouth, where the fingertip lingered, following the trembling curve of her lips, then down to her neck.

She could scarcely breathe; that tormenting, slow caress had made her weak, helpless, wanting him so much it hurt.

Matt bent towards her; his mouth gently touched hers and she groaned in pleasure, her lips parting for him, her eyes tightly shut, her arms going round his neck.

The kiss took fire a second later; they clung like drowning people, hanging on to each other for grim life.

She needed him; he had made her wake up out of the frozen land where her emotions had been trapped all her adult life. He had kissed her awake, like the prince with Sleeping Beauty, and she didn't want to lose him again.

When they slid off the seat on to the petal-strewn grass her eyes flew open in shock, but Matt still kissed her, holding her in his arms, their bodies locked together, and her eyes closed again. She felt the need in him, the desire surging deep inside herself matched by his passion, and gave in to it recklessly, pressing even closer, her breasts hard against his chest, their legs entwined.

Matt ran his seeking fingertips up under her top, she

moaned as he stroked her breasts, her throat dry and hot as she arched up to him, the sweet scent of crushed grass all round them.

Suddenly breaking off his kiss, he buried his face in her throat. 'We can't, not here,' he muttered into her skin. 'Any minute now Lisa is going to come looking for us!'

She was shaking like someone with a high fever. Her hand stroked his hair, warm from the sun, and she gazed up at the blue, blue sky wheeling overhead, knowing she would never forget this moment: the scent of flowers and grass, the sunlight, Matt holding her, kissing her, the wildness in her blood, happiness bubbling up inside her like champagne.

'I'm in love with you,' he whispered. 'I know we've only known each other a very short time, but it happened the minute I saw you walking around the room and I felt almost dizzy watching you. You were so lovely you took my breath away.'

Tears came into her eyes. 'Oh, Matt,' she whispered, hardly daring to believe him. 'Don't say it if you don't mean it; I couldn't bear that.'

'I've never meant anything as much in my life!' he said in a voice that was as deep as the ocean.

She held his face with both hands, looking at him passionately. 'You have to mean it, because I love you, too, more than I can bear! It happened the first day for me, too.' She laughed shakily. 'Love at first sight! I never believed in it, did you?'

It was reckless, dangerous; she knew the risk she was taking, the possibility of loss, of betrayal, of rejection, and accepting them because her love was stronger than her fear.

She would always be grateful to him for bringing her

into the real world, for breaking the ice under which she had lived for so long, for forcing her up into the sunlight and making her feel.

Matt gave a deep groan. 'Darling.' He kissed her mouth hotly, then looked at her with eyes that leapt with desire. 'I badly hoped you felt the same, but you kept running away, and I wasn't sure how you felt about Heston.'

She sighed. 'Honestly, Matt, he was just my boss. I didn't fancy him at all. His constant passes got on my nerves, but it happens all the time, you know. Don isn't the first man in the world to use his power as blackmail, trying to get younger women into bed. I expect it happens in most big companies. A lot of women have to put up with the same thing. What amazes me is that his wife didn't leave him long ago. She must have been through hell.'

Matt's face was sombre. 'I think she has, for years—but for some incredible reason she still loves him. Whether he'll have learnt anything from almost losing her I don't know, but this is his last chance, whether he realises it or not. I believe Sara will divorce him if it ever happens again.'

'He really does care about her; I could see that. It was a terrible shock to him when she asked for a divorce. I've never seen Don in such a state. Let's hope he has learnt a lesson from having to face the possibility of losing her. As far as I'm concerned, I'm leaving the firm as soon as I get another job.'

'Will you come and work for me? I'm not in the business of trying to take over other companies, but you can run our accounts department. I've sacked the previous manager—Sara told me he had been supplying Heston with secret figures on our business. Heston had

promised him that when the take-over happened he
would get a promotion and a lot more money.'

She grimaced. 'Oh, no! I'm so sorry, Matt. Treachery
is always a bitter pill.'

'Yes, it was a shock. Men like Heston remind me of
the snake in the garden of Eden. Everything seems wonderful, then they bring in temptation, and friends turn
into enemies. It leaves a very nasty taste in the mouth.'
He kissed her cheek lingeringly. 'Will you take that
job?'

'I'd love to.'

His smile was like the dawning of the rainbow in a
rainy sky.

'That's wonderful. We can be together all day,
then—drive in together, go home together, to Lisa.'

She looked at him tensely. 'Drive in together?'

'Am I going too fast? I thought you understood...I
want to marry you.'

She drew a painful, shaken breath, green eyes wide
and shimmering. 'Matt, a couple of weeks ago we
hadn't even met!'

'I know. I never thought I'd love again, after my wife
died. I didn't even look at anyone else. I couldn't believe the way you hit me on sight. I thought it was just
the wine I drank over lunch. But then it happened again
the next time I saw you—the same lurch of the heart,
the same breathless excitement.'

She knew just what he meant—she had felt the same
about him.

Matt said huskily, 'The more I saw of you, the deeper
my feelings grew. I knew it was serious from about the
third day. I felt like someone on a bolting horse. I
couldn't stop it, I was helpless; all I could do was let

it happen.' He smiled at her, his lips quivering. 'I want you in a way you wouldn't believe!'

She touched his face with her fingertips, trembling. 'It scares me, to feel this much; I'm afraid it may not last.'

He took her hand and began kissing her fingers, her palm, his mouth hot and passionate.

'I know just how you feel, but we have to trust our own hearts, Bianca. I don't want to spend a night away from you from now on; I want you in my home, in my bed, for ever. Please, say you'll marry me.'

She didn't pretend to have to think, consider. She threw caution and common sense to the wind, not caring about anything but him and the way she loved him.

'I want you, too, very badly. I want to wake up with you beside me and see you sleeping, kiss you awake. I'll live with you or marry you, whatever you want.'

He got to his feet, pulling her up with him, and held both her hands, looking seriously into her eyes.

'Living together isn't enough, not for us. I need you to commit to me, I need to be sure you love me the way I love you, and for me that means marriage. I want you for my wife. Will you marry me, Bianca?'

Gazing back at him, her face calm and certain, she said, 'Yes, Matt. I will.'

A startled sound from the garden path made them both jump and look round. Lisa stood there, in a brief pink sundress, eyes huge, lips parted on a gasp of amazement at what she had just overheard.

Shy and flushed, Bianca held out her hands to her. 'Hello, Lisa! Come and give me a hug.'

Lisa came slowly, as if uncertain how to react, and Bianca picked her up to kiss her.

'You look lovely in that dress; it suits you.'

Looking pleased, Lisa confided, 'Daddy bought it for me in Milan yesterday. We came here in an aeroplane, all the way from London. We had lunch on our laps, like a picnic.'

'That sounds fun. Did you enjoy being on the plane?'

'I was a bit scared, but Daddy held my hand.' Lisa looked at her father, then back at Bianca. 'Are you going to be my mummy?'

Bianca's flush deepened. Huskily she asked, 'Would you like that?' and held her breath, realising that if Lisa rejected her she couldn't marry Matt; she could not hurt his child, or come between them.

But Lisa nodded. 'I always wanted a mummy. When you get married, can I be a bridesmaid?'

Matt looked horrified. 'Do you want bridesmaids?' he asked Bianca.

Lisa's eyes pleaded.

'If I'm getting married, I must have a bridesmaid,' Bianca said, and Lisa beamed, nodding eagerly.

'In a pink dress down to my feet?'

'Yes, and a wreath of pink rosebuds on your head.'

Lisa sighed in ecstasy. 'Will I have my photo taken?'

'Lots of times.'

Matt took Lisa into his own arms. 'When we get back to London, we'll look for a big house for all of us—you, me, and Bianca.'

'Mummy!' she corrected him, then looked uncertainly at Bianca. 'I can call you Mummy, can't I? Then everyone at my new school will know I have a mummy and a daddy.'

Bianca gave Matt a look of enquiry.

'She's starting nursery school when we get back!' he said.

'Oh, that will be exciting,' Bianca told her. 'You'll

be able to make lots of friends. And I'd love you to call me Mummy.'

Lisa had never known her real mother, never lived with her father before. She must often have felt lonely with her grandmother, however much she loved her, however much Matt's mother loved Lisa. All children hate to feel different; they want to be exactly the same as everyone else, wear the same clothes, eat the same food, be part of the gang.

Matt kissed Lisa who put her arms around his neck in a strangling hold then let go and said, 'Put me down, Daddy!'

He did so and she darted off at once, telling then, 'I'm going to tell Aunty Maria about being a bridesmaid.'

Bianca gave a startled cry. 'Oh, but…'

Matt laughed. 'Let her! It will save us the trouble! Lisa loves telling people things; she's a terrible gossip.'

'We'd better go in, too,' Bianca said. 'Before the whole family come rushing out to find us!'

'Not yet,' he whispered, framing her face in his hands. 'I must have another kiss first.' He looked at her with a love that made her heart beat so hard, her whole body trembled with it.

'Oh, Matt,' she breathed, eyes eating his face. 'I do love you.'

He found her mouth with demanding passion and her arms went round his neck, her fingers ran up into his hair, her body clinging to his until they almost seemed to merge, become one, with the hot Italian sun pouring down over them and the future stretching ahead like a golden vision.

Come escape with Harlequin's new
Series Sampler

Four great full-length Harlequin novels bound together in one fabulous volume and at an unbelievable price.

Be transported back in time with a Harlequin Historical® novel, get caught up in a mystery with Intrigue®, be tempted by a hot, sizzling romance with Harlequin Temptation®, or just enjoy a down-home all-American read with American Romance®.

You won't be able to put this collection down!

On sale February 2000 at your favorite retail outlet.

HARLEQUIN®
Makes any time special ™

Visit us at www.romance.net   PHESC

Return to the charm of the Regency era with

GEORGETTE
HEYER,

creator of the modern Regency genre.

Enjoy six romantic collector's editions with forewords
by some of today's bestselling romance authors,

**Nora Roberts, Mary Jo Putney,
Jo Beverley, Mary Balogh,
Theresa Medeiros and Kasey Michaels.**

Frederica
On sale February 2000

The Nonesuch
On sale March 2000

The Convenient Marriage
On sale April 2000

Cousin Kate
On sale May 2000

The Talisman Ring
On sale June 2000

The Corinthian
On sale July 2000

Available at your favorite retail outlet.

HARLEQUIN®
Makes any time special ™

Back by popular demand are

DEBBIE MACOMBER's

Hard Luck, Alaska, is a
town that needs women!
And the O'Halloran brothers
are just the fellows
to fly them in.

Starting in March 2000 this beloved series returns
in special 2-in-1 collector's editions:

MAIL-ORDER MARRIAGES, featuring
Brides for Brothers and *The Marriage Risk*
On sale March 2000

FAMILY MEN, featuring
Daddy's Little Helper and *Because of the Baby*
On sale July 2000

THE LAST TWO BACHELORS, featuring
Falling for Him and *Ending in Marriage*
On sale August 2000

Collect and enjoy each MIDNIGHT SONS story!

Available at your favorite retail outlet.

HARLEQUIN®
Makes any time special ™

Visit us at www.romance.net

PHMS